DESTINY

VALENTINE'S ON EMERALD MOUNTAIN

CARA MALONE

Copyright © 2022 by Cara Malone

All rights reserved.

No part of this book may be reproduced in any form or by any electronic or mechanical means, including information storage and retrieval systems, without written permission from the author, except for the use of brief quotations in a book review.

1
HALEY

The air was crisp and thin on Emerald Mountain.

Haley had stepped off the plane at the airport feeling grumpy and tired. The altitude, not extreme but higher than she was used to, hadn't done much for the exhaustion, but by the time she arrived at Emerald Mountain Ski Resort, she couldn't help feeling happier.

It was February first and winter was still in full force here, with a thick blanket of snow on the ground and big flakes falling serenely from the coated evergreens. All around her were blissful vacationers and quite a few lovey-dovey couples. That was the whole reason for her trip – she wasn't among the lovey-dovey, but she was here to document their romantic adventures, along with her best friend Val.

The two of them worked for *Traverse,* a travel magazine out of Chicago. Val was the writer of the duo, and Haley took the pictures. For the last couple of years, they'd been an unstoppable team traveling the country and writing the magazine's most popular features. And for the next two weeks, they were in Emerald Mountain to document the Valentine's Day festivities here.

It was only a little unfortunate that V-Day happened to be Haley's least favorite holiday. And that Val hadn't shut up about her girlfriend for the entire three-hour flight.

"I just don't get why it's such a big deal if I bring Moska with me," she was saying as they made their way through the enormous main lodge to the check-in desk. "It's not like I wanted Art to foot the bill."

Art was their boss, and the definition of stodgy despite being the magazine's creative director. In the two years Haley had been at *Traverse,* she got the impression that Art was waging a private war in which he was the only participant. Old guard versus upstart new staff members, bent on changing things and ruining the magazine's traditions.

Drag me out back and shoot me if I ever get like that, Haley had whispered to Val after many a staff meeting.

Of course, she would never admit to Val that she

was secretly pleased Art had stonewalled her attempts to bring her girlfriend along on this particular trip. Haley wasn't thrilled about two whole weeks of being surrounded by couples, photographing romantic activities at a resort that was attempting to become a destination for lovers. As much as Haley liked Moska, if she had to be the third wheel between her and Val, she really would beg to be dragged out back and put down.

"You know how Art is," Haley said, the perfect mix of vague and supportive. Then she pulled out her company credit card and passed it across the check-in counter. "Hi, we're with *Traverse* magazine – Haley Thomas and Valerie Cross."

The concierge's eyes lit up with recognition. "My manager told me to be on the lookout for you. He upgraded you to a private cabin, and he asked to meet you, if you don't mind."

"Sure," Haley said. They were used to this kind of celebrity treatment – it was one of the major perks of the job – and making nice with the staff was part of the deal.

The song and dance took about twenty minutes. The manager, a forty-something man named Greg who wasn't unlike Art, relieved them of their luggage and gave them a tour of the expansive lodge. It had great views of the mountain from floor-to-ceiling windows, and Greg pointed out multiple additional buildings for ski rentals, an après ski lounge, and various other activities. Haley made some mental notes about shots she'd want to come back for, when the lighting was right, and Val had her little reporter's notebook out, scribbling details as they walked.

At last, Greg brought them back to the front desk, where their swipe cards were waiting along with a bellhop.

"There's a schedule of events waiting in your cabin, along with a complimentary bottle of champagne and my cell number," he told them. "And Ivan here will take you to the cabin. If you have any questions or special requests, please don't hesitate to contact me."

Haley exchanged a glance with Val – even for someone hoping to get a good review, Greg was laying it on thick. Ivan, who looked like he was about twelve but also tall enough to play professional basketball, led them outside to a waiting utility vehicle that looked like a golf cart on steroids.

Thankfully, Ivan hadn't gotten the memo about kissing Haley and Val's butts, and the ride down the main road to a row of log cabins was much more comfortable. Well, if you didn't count the near-zero-degree wind blasting Haley in the face from the wide-open vehicle. Still, she much preferred natural conversation with the staff over the ones that were hell-bent on schmoozing her.

"Here we are, ladies," Ivan said, coming to a skidding stop in front of cabin number seven. "I'll get your bags."

"We can take them," Val offered.

Ivan shook his head. "Uncle Greg would kick my ass."

Ah, so that explained this fresh-faced, slightly foul-mouthed kid's presence on the staff. Haley let herself into the cabin, where she found not only a bottle of champagne but a dozen red roses, a cannister of expensive hot cocoa mix, and a pair of mascarpone-stuffed, chocolate-covered strawberries each the size of her fist. Val tipped Ivan as soon as he'd unloaded their luggage in the entryway, and came over to Haley in the kitchen.

"Wow, do you think Greg wants to fuck us or the magazine?" she asked.

"I 'on't really care," Haley said, her mouth stuffed with the most delicious strawberry she'd ever tasted. She swallowed. "But if it's us, you're gonna have to take one for the team. You're at least bi, I don't play that sport at all."

"You're the one who's single. What am I supposed to tell Moska about 'taking one for the team'?"

"Bring her your strawberry and she'll forgive you," Haley said with a smirk. "It's incredible."

Val turned to explore the cabin, laughing over her shoulder. "You can eat mine if I can have first pick of the rooms."

"Deal," Haley said, already reaching for the second strawberry. She really should have photographed this welcome display, but the fact that she'd forgotten was merely an excuse to call down to the lodge and request more strawberries.

"This place is big enough for us both to have brought someone!" Val pouted from one of the bedrooms.

Haley rolled her eyes and picked up the event schedule. Her last girlfriend had ground her heart into a thousand pieces – Haley was hardly going to invite *her* on a two-week trip. Val was her best friend and she was already here. So who did that leave for Haley to bring on a romantic getaway, her mom?

She scanned through the events. A sunrise hike, couple's massages, wine tasting, stargazing, all sorts of classes designed for two – painting, skiing, cooking, dancing. Okay, so maybe Art was being a bit of a dick when he told Val she couldn't bring her girlfriend on this assignment. How was she supposed to write about all this couple stuff from the sidelines?

Val appeared around the corner of the kitchen. "I'm sorry I keep talking about Moska... it's just that this is our first Valentine's Day living in the same state, let alone the same apartment, and I can't believe we're still not spending it together."

"I get it."

"Am I being annoying?"

"When are you not?"

"Butt." Val came over and wrapped her arms around Haley. "I'll shut up about her if you want me to."

Haley rolled her eyes again. "No, I'm happy that you're happy. It's fine."

Val kissed her cheek. "Thanks." Then she perked up and released Haley. "Okay, well, there's a Jacuzzi tub in the bathroom and it's got an incredible view. I'm gonna go have a bubble bath and call her."

"In that case, I think I'll go for a walk before you figure out how to sit on the jets," Haley said. "I love you, but I don't want to hear that."

"You have such a filthy mind," Val chastised. "I just want to let her know we landed safely."

"Right," Haley answered, unconvinced.

Val had met Moska on an assignment shortly before Haley got hired at the magazine. She'd been in New York City covering their Diwali celebration and wound up spending the whole weekend in bed, falling in love and having crazy monkey sex. It had taken Moska two whole years to save up the money, find a job and move to Chicago for Val, and they'd been inseparable ever since. Nauseating, but adorable.

Haley heard a tap turn on somewhere deeper in the cabin, and she went to her carry-on bag by the front door. She'd explore their accommodations later – right now she wanted to give Val some space and get acquainted with the resort before she lost all the natural light for the day. She found her camera and selected a standard lens, then called, "I'm headed out – say hi to Moska for me!"

"Will do!" Val called back, then Haley was out the door.

It was late afternoon, well past the golden hour, so she likely wouldn't get any shots that actually made it into the magazine. But it would be helpful to take some test shots that she could review on her laptop, then go back for better photos later.

She got to the end of the short sidewalk in front of her cabin and paused, looking around. There were nearly two dozen private cabins all lined up in a row on a semi-plowed road. Number seven was basically right in the middle. Down the road to her left was the main lodge and the other buildings Greg had pointed out. And to her right, there were the ski slopes, the hiking paths, and the big, wild mountains beyond.

The sight was breathtaking, the scale intimidating. The longer she stared at the mountains stretching impossibly into the distance, the smaller she felt. The more alone.

So when her toes started to feel numb and she knew she needed to move, Haley chose to go left – toward civilization. She walked gingerly, because as clear as the road was, there were still slick patches of ice here and there. If she fell, she'd choose to break her ass before she let anything happen to her camera, so not falling at all was best.

"No wonder they drive monster-truck golf carts around here," she mumbled to herself as she got her footing and braved a few photographs of the resort from a distance.

There were people milling about, mostly clustered around the resort where the rest of the hotel rooms were. No one else was on this road and Haley started to wonder if she was supposed to call Ivan to drive her back and forth every time she wanted to leave her cabin. Not that she would have – she wasn't afraid of a little ice.

Besides, she thought with a smirk, *I'm a travel photographer – I go where I want*.

Okay, so maybe the special treatment had gone to her head just a wee bit.

She got her balance and took more pictures as she meandered toward the resort, using the perfect quiet of the mountain to steel herself for the romantic events of the two weeks ahead of her. She passed a few people the closer to the resort she got – mostly couples, but a few families with their children. All exceedingly heterosexual-looking.

Speed dating was one of the activities Haley had spotted on the schedule, and she was curious what kind of single person would choose to vacation at a resort designed for couples on Valentine's Day. She'd have to go to the event to take pictures anyway so she was looking forward to finding out, but it appeared that whatever else the answer included, it would also be 'a straight single person.'

Haley got a few more good shots before the afternoon faded into twilight, and then she just wandered. It was getting cold – her nose feeling more like a popsicle than something attached to the rest of her – and she was just about to turn back when she reached the entrance to the resort. There wasn't anywhere else to go from here anyway, other than out to the highway, but she paused before turning around.

On a ladder about twelve feet in the air, a woman in heavy-duty coveralls struggled to hang a string of pink and red twinkle lights from the resort's entry arch. Haley smiled. It was definitely a job for two, but she recognized the look of stubborn determination in the woman's face. It was something Haley would do, too.

She thought about offering to help. Would that be

an insult to the woman's independence, or an invitation to be groveled to as Greg had? *Oh, Miss Thomas, of course we wouldn't put you to work – except on taking beautiful photos of our lovely resort, wink, wink.*

So instead of helping, Haley lifted her camera again, hoping there was enough light left to capture the moment. This wasn't a photo for the magazine – it was just for her.

As she zoomed in, she noticed the woman's plump lower lip, the way it jutted out in a pout of frustration, and the frown lines of extreme concentration between her brows. A strand of bright teal hair stuck unexpectedly out of her beanie and made Haley curious about the rest of her 'do. This woman was cute and androgynous and at least a little rebellious in exactly the way Haley was attracted to. She wondered what she'd look like without those bulky coveralls.

Well, in normal clothes, she thought. *That's what I meant.*

Sure you did, her darker, snarkier side shot back.

She let her camera hang around her neck again – the only thing worse than getting caught watching and not helping would be getting caught snapping candids. She opened her mouth to call out to the woman, to offer help after all, when a car with skis strapped to the hood took the turn off the highway too fast and started skidding right for the arch.

2

DES

"Look out!"

Someone screamed, and in the next second, Des felt the ladder disappearing from under her feet. She didn't think – she just bear-hugged the arch in front of her and squeezed her eyes shut, waiting to come crashing down.

"Oh my God!" the same voice shouted, but Des was still securely clinging to the arch, wide as a telephone pole and thankfully sturdy. She heard a loud thump a few yards off and hazarded a peek. There was a car nose-deep in a snowbank beside the road, and a woman in a crimson coat not far away. Des's ladder lay in the snow.

"Are you okay?" the woman called up to Des.

"Yeah, fine," Des said, hooking her ankles to secure her hold. "What about them?"

She nodded toward the car, where the driver's door flew open. A bewildered man stepped out, seeming more concerned about the front end of his car than the employee he'd nearly obliterated. "Oh gosh, the roads are slippery today!" he said. "Jeez, how'm I gonna dig out of that?"

The woman in the red coat went over to him. "Are you okay, sir? What about your passengers?"

"Yeah, we're all okay," he said, then leaned back into the car. "Kids, get out here and help me dig."

Crimson Coat came back to Des. "I can't put your ladder back up – it's broken."

"Aww, shit." Des wasn't a huge fan of heights, especially when there was no ladder, but it wasn't a phobia she was willing to admit to – especially to attractive little snow bunnies.

"Can you slide down, like a fireman's pole?" the woman called. "I'll catch you."

Now, there was a tasty bit of motivation. For a few seconds, her ego waged a battle between asking Crimson Coat to step back so she could land with an impressive dismount – if she was lucky – and taking the opportunity to fall into a hot woman's arms. Usually it was the other way around, but Des wasn't opposed to switching it up every now and then.

In the end, necessity won out. Her coveralls weren't the grippiest of wardrobe choices and her bare hands were starting to freeze in the elements. So she decided on a controlled drop that ended with Crimson Coat's arms wrapped around her, body pressed against her back.

She twisted around, disappointed when the woman released her quickly. "Thanks. I'm Des."

"Haley," her knight in eiderdown armor replied.

She was even cuter up close, with a heart-shaped face and gray-blue eyes, and blonde ringlets poking out of the bottom of her knit cap. Not only that, the look she was giving Des was one of unmistakable desire.

Score.

Des had been working at the resort since the end of summer and the constantly rotating supply of eye candy was one of her favorite aspects of the job. There were a lot of tens on Emerald Mountain. Unfortunately, the vast majority she'd talked to had turned out to be straight and/or taken. She certainly wasn't banking on meeting any single queer women during the resort's Valentine's celebrations… but it seemed like she might be getting lucky after all.

In every sense of the word, if she played her cards right.

"Excuse me?" Another female voice interrupted Des as she silently thanked the vacation fling gods. This one was not nearly so sweet and alluring. "Are you going to help us or what?"

Des looked over Haley's shoulder to the snowbound car. The matriarch had managed to haul herself out of it and was standing with her hands on her hips in the traditional *I'd like to speak to the manager* stance.

Ah, yes. The other common subgroup of guests, the one that made Des want to quit without notice some days.

"Let me call the grounds crew," Des said, reaching for the walkie clipped to her belt. She radioed it in, then added, "They'll get you out of there in a jiffy."

Jiffy. Sometimes Des didn't know who she was anymore, but she'd picked those types of words up from the likes of Greg, and they really did wonders on guests like this woman, who'd probably manage to get her room comped because her husband crashed his own car.

"Or you could, you know, lift a finger?" the woman said. Incredible.

Des just laughed internally, but Haley stepped forward. Her face had gone surprisingly red as she told the woman, "You know, some people would apologize when they nearly kill someone and damage private property."

The woman's mouth dropped into a perfectly round O and it was one of the most satisfying things Des had experienced since she started working there.

She was still standing so close to Haley she could feel her body heat, and she whispered in her ear, "Can I hire you to walk around and say what I'm thinking?"

Then she reluctantly snapped back into *employee who doesn't want to lose her job* mode.

She stepped around Haley, getting between her and the entitled guest. "The grounds crew will be here any second and they'll have you on your way, I promise."

"Who is that?" the woman asked, pointing at Haley. "I want her name!"

"She's not an employee," Des said. "Why don't you all wait inside your car where it's warm, and I'll make sure there's some hot cocoa waiting for you when you get to your room?"

There, they didn't even have to speak to a manager for that small perk. Des hated herself a little bit in that moment, but it got the woman to stuff herself indignantly back into the passenger seat of her car. Des turned to Haley.

"You better get out of here before she decides to include you in her Yelp review," she said, earning a chuckle. "Thanks for your help."

Haley nodded. "Any time." She gave Des a little half smile that warmed her up better than any cup of hot cocoa, and then she sauntered off, back the way she'd come. Was it Des's imagination or was she putting a little extra sway in her hips?

Damn, Des couldn't wait to run into her again.

She heard the rumble of a utility vehicle approaching on a side road, and another impatient voice. "Destiny! What happened here?"

Ugh. Greg, on the other hand... let's just say he wasn't the most beloved manager Des had ever worked for. The job was full of ups and downs. The ability to set her own pace and figure out her own way to solve a problem were upsides, along with the free skiing and all the beautiful women. Greg, well, he was a downside.

For instance, how many times did she have to tell him that even though her legal name was Destiny, nobody called her that?

He hopped off the UTV while two members of the grounds crew set about hooking up a tow rope to the car. Greg came over to Des, still zipping up his coat. He was always moving, appearing around every corner and sticking his nose in every little problem around the resort. Des could never decide if that was dedication to his job, or if he was just checking up on everyone because he didn't trust them.

Don't take it personal, he's just insecure, her friend, Joy, had said the last time Des complained about him. *He's a micromanager.*

Joy was a former employee, and a native of nearby Emerald Hill like Des. She'd already moved on from the resort by the time Des started working here, but she'd helped Des get the interview for her maintenance job. And even though she'd been gone over four years, she still insisted the resort was a great place to work once you figured out its quirks.

Or figured out how to get Greg fired, Des had mused at the time.

"You haven't finished hanging the lights?" he said now, not bothering to let her answer his initial question. "Destiny, you know there's a storm coming – I want those hung before we get even more snow."

"I was working on it when the car crashed," Des said. "They broke the ladder–"

"And we're just glad no one is hurt!" Greg said, raising his voice. One thing he couldn't stand was the suggestion that any resort guest had ever done anything wrong, and Des should have known better than to phrase it like that.

"I'll ride back with the grounds crew and get another ladder," she said.

Greg frowned. What now?

"I was going to have them drop me back at the lodge," he said, looking to the car being winched out of the snowbank. "Ordinarily I'd walk back and let them drop you off, but I really need to be there when these folks check in."

"I promised them hot cocoa in their room for their trouble," Des said.

"Good idea," Greg answered, a rare pleased expression on his face. Then he added, mumbling to himself, "Better give them a room upgrade too if possible."

"You know they almost took out me, my ladder and the archway, right?" Des said.

"What?"

"Never mind," she answered. "I'll go get another ladder."

She set off on foot. It would take longer, but a snowy walk at twilight wasn't the worst thing in the world. The scenery and the seclusion were some of the best things about Emerald Mountain. She'd grown up on those slopes, and lived her whole life in this area. It was home and she couldn't imagine feeling this comfortable anywhere else.

Except maybe on top of Crimson Coat, aka Haley – although that was a whole different kind of good feeling.

3
HALEY

When she got back to the cabin, Haley was surprised to hear arguing.

She walked down the short hall that led to the bedrooms, taking in the space for the first time as she peeked into a couple rooms looking for Val. Large, luxurious bathroom still humid from Val's soak. One bedroom with large bay windows that looked perfect for curling up with a book and a blanket. And another bedroom, strewn with Val's luggage, her best friend pacing the floor in the center of it all.

"I get that, baby, and I'm sorry you're going to be alone on Valentine's Day," she was saying into her phone. "But you know how hard I tried with Art, and don't you think *I'm* going to feel left out if you go to that party?"

Haley had left the scene at the entrance to the resort feeling surprisingly lovey-dovey, bewitched by Des's broad smile and confidence. She'd practically floated back to the cabin on a sea of ridiculous fantasies her mind conjured all on its own – all the different ways Cupid's arrow could strike her on this trip and let her have some fun with that gorgeous woman.

Now, watching Val bicker with her girlfriend, the sea drained from beneath Haley's feet and she came back to earth. Oh right, this is what real-life romance is like.

You okay? she mouthed when Val noticed her standing in the doorway.

Val rolled her eyes and put Moska on speakerphone. "Haley, don't you think it's weird to go to a Valentine's party without your significant other?"

"You're out of town!" Moska shot back. "It's not like I'm bringing a date. Haley, tell her she's being ridiculous."

"Hell no," Haley said, holding her hands up. "You know my policy on getting involved in other people's relationships."

It happened to be the same as her policy on getting into relationships of her own – she just didn't do it anymore. It was never worth it, and when she tried, she only ended up getting hurt.

"Good luck with that," she said, then told Val she was going to her room to unpack.

She left the two of them fighting, went to the living room to retrieve her luggage, and before she even reached her bedroom door, she could hear the two of them simultaneously apologizing over speakerphone.

"I just got jealous," Val was saying.

"And I hate being apart from you," Moska answered.

Haley rolled her eyes as she went into her room and closed the door behind her. Val was five years younger than her, and most of the time it didn't show. She was a hell of a writer and Haley didn't know anyone at *Traverse* who had a stronger work ethic. But when it came to romance, it was very obvious that she was a sweetly naïve twenty-three-year-old.

Haley turned on some music on her phone to drown out the drama, then unpacked her bags. She was mostly concerned with the tech she'd brought, making sure nothing had been lost or damaged along the way. But she was a careful packer and this wasn't her first rodeo, so to speak, so everything was exactly as she'd left it.

She was sitting in the window seat, wrapped in the plush robe she'd found hanging in the closet, uploading the photos from the afternoon to her computer when Val knocked. "Come in," she called.

"You look cozy."

"This spot's really comfy but it's like, twenty degrees out there," Haley explained. "The window's really cold."

"Wanna make hot cocoa and see if we can get the fireplace going?" Val asked. "Or we can pop the champagne if you're in the mood."

"I think Greg will be disappointed if we don't invite him to join in," Haley joked, closing her laptop. "You and Moska okay?"

"Yeah, we worked through it," Val said with a sigh. "I hate feeling jealous whenever I get left out – which is often thanks to the magazine."

"I hear that," Haley said, even though she had no interest in acquiring some relationship drama of her own. She'd had more than enough of that in her life, and was starting to think of the magazine as her significant other. *God, that's sad,* she thought as she went into the kitchen. "Cocoa or champagne?"

"Mmm, cocoa tonight," Val said. "We'll save the champagne for when we really need it."

Val went to the gas fireplace along one wall in the spacious open-concept living area. Haley started some water boiling on the stove, then asked, "Do you think it's worth it?"

"What?"

"Love."

Val looked at her like she had snakes for hair.

Haley hurried to add, "I mean, it just seems like you and Moska spend a lot of time worrying about what would happen if you didn't have each other. All I'm saying is maybe it's less stressful to be single."

"Maybe, but who said it's a bad thing to worry about losing each other?" Val said. "Yes, Moska and I fight sometimes, but it's because we love each other so damn much. She drives me up the wall sometimes but I'd walk through fire for that woman."

Haley came over with two cups of cocoa. "Maybe I just haven't loved the right person yet."

"I guarantee that's true, or else I wouldn't have to explain all this to you," Val said, taking one of the mugs. She pointed to the fireplace. "I can't figure this stupid thing out. There are no igniter buttons anywhere."

Haley set down her mug and looked around a minute, then flipped a switch on the wall. A blue flame ignited in the fireplace and Val gave her a sardonic look.

"I thought that was for the lights."

"What can I say, I'm a genius," Haley answered, then picked out a spot in a big, plush armchair. She was still wearing the resort robe, and she drew her knees to her chest as she settled in with her cocoa. It was about as snuggly and warm as she'd ever remembered feeling and the only thing that could make it better was another body there in the armchair – preferably that of a tall, lean, teal-haired woman.

Oh my God, why do you want to bang her so much? her subconscious asked when she realized she was fantasizing about Des again. *Talk about lust at first sight.*

Well, the looks she was giving me said she wouldn't be opposed, she thought. Then she heard herself blurt, "I met someone while I was on my walk."

"Ooh, explain," Val said, leaning over the arm of the couch where she was sitting, rapt.

Immediately, Haley regretted her words. When had her mouth decided to betray her like that? "I mean I met one of the staff members," she corrected. "She was stringing lights for the Valentine's festivities. Got a couple good shots, so maybe we can use them in the article, talk about how much work goes into the resort's events."

Val just stared at her like she was completely transparent. "Bullshit."

"What?"

"You said that in such a dreamy voice – I don't think I've ever heard that tone from you before," she said, then imitated Haley. "*I met someone on my walk.*"

"I did not say it like that!" Haley pouted.

"Did you give her your number?" Val asked. "Or at least tell her what cabin you're staying in? Should I make other sleeping arrangements?"

"Shut up," Haley said, then pulled a throw pillow from behind her back and chucked it at Val, avoiding a hot cocoa disaster only because she had terrible aim.

Okay, so maybe their maturity levels were closer than she liked to admit.

"Fine, we don't have to talk about the staff member you're *madly in love with*," Val teased. "But promise me one thing?"

"What?"

"Keep an open mind," Val said. "I know you're all 'love stinks' and you think it's not for you because of your rotten ex, but we got sent out to cover a Valentine's event. You're gonna have a lot more fun the next two weeks if you let yourself believe in the spirit of the season."

"I don't think love stinks," Haley said, lying through her teeth. At length she added, "But okay… in the name of business."

Val laughed. "Hallelujah – Haley Thomas opens herself up to the possibility of love, but only for corporate gain! I'll alert Art, he'll be thrilled."

"Don't you dare tell Art about my love life," Haley shot back.

Val gave her a challenging look. "What's to tell?"

"Ooh, ouch," Haley answered, then dove into her hot cocoa mug because that burn was a little too honest to really be funny.

4
DES

The next morning, there was a weekly staff meeting. Des did her best to stick to the back of the room, near the table of donuts and coffee and out of Greg's line of sight. She really didn't want to hear what he had to say about the car accident yesterday afternoon, especially after the family had a chance to give him their side of the story.

With Des's luck, the matriarch had found a way to make the whole thing her fault – her ladder was sticking out into the road or her brightly colored, non-traditional hairstyle had so startled her husband that it caused him to crash.

In general, Des had been pretty quick to catch on to the fact that it was best to stay under Greg's radar. His nephew, Ivan, knew that lesson well and could be counted on to hide in the back with Des.

"How's it going in the lodge this season?" she asked him while she cream-and-sugared her coffee and waited for the meeting to start. "Ready to go to college yet?"

"Nah, Uncle Greg's a pain sometimes but it's better than four more years of school," Ivan said, selecting an enormous cinnamon swirl donut.

He'd told Des a while back that was the deal his family had given him after he graduated high school: go to work for Uncle Greg, or get his degree. Ivan wanted to be a pro snowboarder, so it seemed like working at a resort with great slopes was the better choice. Des had a soft spot for the kid because, even though he was young and dumb like all eighteen-year-olds, he had a lot of heart.

And maybe his parents' ultimatum reminded her a bit of her own teenage years. She'd made a different choice – to move out and live her own life – but her parents had been asking for more of a sacrifice than just going to college. They'd wanted her to be someone she wasn't, and that was never going to happen.

"Okay, everyone, let's get started," Greg called from the front of the room.

Des popped a lid on her coffee cup then sat down behind a couple of tall kitchen staff members, listening and hoping not to be seen.

For the next half hour, Greg ran down the list of

activities the resort had planned for its two-week Valentine's extravaganza, making sure everything was in order right down to the lavender massage oil the spa had ordered for its couples massage offering.

"Is Destiny Grove here?" Greg called, craning his neck to look around. "Did you finish hanging the twinkle lights?"

She rolled her eyes. Of course he couldn't simply trust her to do what she said she would... or even use his eyeballs when he drove in this morning, apparently. She leaned around one of the cooks and called, "Yeah, they're up."

"Good, good," Greg said, checking them off the clipboard he was reading from.

"Would it kill him to say 'thanks'?" Ivan whispered beside her, and Des snorted.

"Probably."

Greg finished running down his checklist, then reminded everyone that there were a couple of journalists from *Traverse* magazine here covering the festivities for the next two weeks. As if anyone could forget – it was practically all he could talk about ever since they agreed to come.

Emerald Mountain used to be just your typical ski destination, popular for winter vacations and Christmas getaways. Then *Traverse* came two years ago in the winter and did a holiday feature that did the print magazine equivalent of going viral. The resort had been booked solid through December last year, and the owners wanted to capitalize on its newfound fame.

So now they were doing everything they could to cater to vacationers on every holiday, and Valentine's Day was going to be their next big attraction. Des had a sneaking suspicion Greg had a bonus riding on the event's success. He certainly was acting like his life depended on it, and getting *Traverse* to come back had been a huge feather in his cap.

"Oh, and one more thing before I let you all go," he said, checking the time. Nearly forty-five minutes past Des's usual starting time, but she was on the clock already so he could talk all day as far as she was concerned. "The National Weather Service is calling for a severe winter storm tonight – it could even get upgraded to a blizzard. Don't cause any panic, but alert guests as you see them and be ready to batten down the hatches." He gave a sharp clap that echoed through the room, waking up anyone who'd dared doze off. "All right, people, get out there and make someone's day!"

That was one of a few of Greg's cheesy expressions Des actually liked. Joy told her he was saying it way back when he was just a shift manager, and it actually translated to an improvement in the resort's Yelp scores. For those employees who were the type of people who cared about that kind of thing.

Everyone was moving toward the door now, and Des joined the herd. She'd nearly succeeded in slipping out unnoticed when she heard her name.

"Destiny, can you hang back?" Greg called.

Damn it. Time to get chewed out for not hurling her body in front of those guests' skidding car yesterday.

She sidestepped out of the flow of traffic and met Greg at the front of the room. He was absorbed in his checklist, and Des noticed a penciled-in item at the bottom of the page. She couldn't make out most of Greg's tiny handwriting, but she did see her name.

"Our guests in cabin twenty alerted us that a branch fell on their roof in the night," he said. "The grounds crew took a look and said there's likely shingle damage. I need you to tarp it before that storm hits. The last thing we need is a leaky roof and big repairs."

"No problem," Des said. "Is it still occupied?"

"No, I moved the guests to number nineteen for the rest of their stay, and twenty isn't booked again until February fourth."

"I'll get right on it," Des promised.

She started to walk away and he asked, "How are you doing on your other tasks?"

He was referring to the obscenely long to-do list he'd given her department to prepare the resort for Valentine's Day. Most of it was décor-related, and some of it involved moving furniture and setting up for stuff like the couples' cooking class. As one of only three members of the maintenance crew, and the only one that worked the day shift, most of it fell on Des's shoulders.

Besides that, she suspected Greg was looking for an excuse to get rid of her before her six-month probation ended. She spoke her mind, especially when she first got here, and he didn't like people who had opinions of their own.

"It'll all get done on time," she promised. She wasn't getting fired simply for failing to move some damn tables.

Before Greg had a chance to pile on anything more, she flashed him her cheesiest, most reassuring grin and headed out the door. She pulled out her phone, where she had recorded the unending list of tasks Greg had given her, and added cabin twenty's roof to the list.

The day turned out to be a long and tedious one, where every project Des tried to complete came with unforeseen problems and setbacks. Each time she tried to cross off something simple, it turned out to require three more mini tasks before it could be finished.

And all day long, she had Greg on her walkie. "Destiny, are you finished moving the tables for the speed dating event? Destiny, a lodge guest's thermostat isn't working, please fix that ASAP. Destiny, please update me on how many items on your list are still outstanding." The guy cared about this resort more than Des cared about most anything, but lord, he was the king of micromanagement.

She actually had a pretty productive day in spite of him, but cabin twenty's roof kept getting pushed down the list. It was nearly five o'clock and quitting time when she realized she still hadn't gotten out there to tarp it, and she knew she couldn't leave it. It wouldn't be safe for the night crew to work in the dark, and that damn winter storm was coming soon. She could already see the sky starting to turn a telltale gray.

"Welp, somebody's getting a little overtime pay," she said to herself as she went to the maintenance building to gather the supplies she'd need. At least Greg wasn't stingy with payroll.

She loaded a UTV with a ladder, a small tarp, and a toolbox, then drove over to the row of luxury cabins. As she went, she spotted a familiar crimson coat on the road ahead of her, and smiled to herself. She hadn't forgotten about Haley – it was damn near impossible to forget a woman whose hips had been pressed her ass against within minutes of meeting her, and those light blue eyes the color of a clear mountain sky were equally memorable.

But damn it all, the light was quickly fading from the sky, and Des knew snow clouds when she saw them. By her estimate, she had about half an hour to get up on that roof and do the job before she lost the light. Who knew if the storm would hold out that long?

She couldn't stop to talk to Crimson Coat, not even just to say hi. She knew how hard it was to tear herself away from a beautiful woman – she'd end up missing her window of opportunity to tarp the roof and then Greg would have a conniption fit.

Des had no choice but to drive right past Haley, but she did give the vehicle's horn a quick double-tap on her way by. Haley turned her head and Des winked at her. She had just enough time to catch the smile of recognition on Haley's face before she had to look at the road again.

Worth it.

Cabin twenty was the very last one in the row,

which meant it was the most secluded and it also had an unobstructed, stunning view of the mountain. There was no one on the ski slopes thanks to the incoming storm, so being up on the roof by herself, Des felt like the only person in the world.

It was peaceful, beautiful, and more than a little eerie with the heavy storm clouds hanging overhead.

She threw the fallen branch off the side of the roof and worked as quickly as she could to secure a tarp over the damaged shingles. An actual repair would have to wait until the weather warmed and things were less hectic around the resort, but this would hold in the meantime.

Big, wet snowflakes started to fall before Des was finished. The ladder rungs were slippery as she carefully climbed down to the ground, and by the time she had the ladder loaded back onto the UTV, those big flakes had turned into a flurry. She looked up the road and could barely see the next cabin in the row. That was how it happened around here – perfect visibility to white-out conditions in only a few minutes. Being in the valley beneath looming mountains didn't help.

Visibility was low, but this was far from Des's first snowstorm. She could have made it back to the maintenance shed if she wanted to – though it would be a white-knuckle trip, and the UTV was open to the elements so it'd be a cold one too.

What was waiting for her there, though? Greg, with a cup of hot cocoa and a pat on the back for a job well done? Hardly. She'd clock out only to endure another white-knuckle drive into Emerald Hill, back to her empty apartment. It didn't even have a fireplace, which cabin twenty did. She grabbed her walkie, tuning into the lodge channel.

"Hey, this is Des Grove, anybody listening? Over."

"I hear you, Des," came a familiar voice, one of the shift supervisors. "What's up? Over."

"Greg had me fixing the roof on cabin twenty," she said. "It's done, but I can't get back to the lodge in the storm." That was a fib, but she was already fantasizing about a cozy night of luxury in front of the fireplace. "I'm gonna hole up here for the night, over."

"You want someone to come out and get you? Over."

Hell no, that was the last thing she wanted. "I'll be fine – I'll check in in the morning, thanks. Over and out."

She secured her tools in the lockable storage compartment in the back of the UTV, then turned to go into the cabin – but something in the storm caught her eye. Something bright red. She turned back toward the road, squinting into the snow.

"Haley?" She shouted but there was no answer.

She cupped her hands around her mouth and tried again. "Can you hear me?"

"Somebody there?" The answer was faint, the storm stealing the power of the woman's voice, but Des knew she wasn't imagining it now. Haley had gotten caught in the storm just like Des, but unlike her, she wasn't used to it, didn't know how to navigate through it.

"I'm coming!" Des called.

She had to lean into the wind to get to her. The snowflakes, big and pretty just a few minutes ago, were now tiny and stinging and plentiful as they slapped her face. She squinted into them as she trudged up the road and met Haley.

"You okay?" she said, having to raise her voice even standing a few feet from the woman.

Haley's face was swallowed up in the enormous, fur-lined hood of her coat, but Des could see how red her nose and cheeks were. "I got turned around."

"It happens," she said. Thankfully, not very often. "Which cabin is yours?"

"Seven," Haley told her.

Des frowned. She could just see the outlines of cabins eighteen and nineteen from where they stood, and even with the UTV, it wouldn't be a fun journey getting her home.

Besides... her fantasy about the fireplace was

already starting to evolve to include Haley. They'd had chemistry the other day, and that smile Haley gave her when Des passed earlier was more than friendly acknowledgement. She decided to go for it.

"Too far," she said. "You better come with me."

"Where?" Haley shouted over the storm, which was thick enough now to be classified as a full-on blizzard.

"Cabin twenty," Des said. "It's empty, we can shelter there for the night."

If all they ended up doing was huddling by the fire for warmth, so be it. If something more happened... so much the better.

Haley nodded assent and Des grabbed her gloved hand. The wind was at their backs now, which made things easier. They made their way to the last cabin in the row and Des used the universal keycard clipped to her employee badge to get in – the perks of being on the maintenance crew.

Snow blew in with them and Des actually had to wrestle the door closed. Once she did, though, the silence and stillness of the cabin enveloped them, and she let out a relieved breath.

"Are storms always this bad out here?" Haley asked.

Des shook her head. "The weather service has been forecasting this will be one of the worst we've had in years. I wouldn't be surprised if we have a foot of snow by the time it's over."

Haley smiled. "That actually sounds like fun. I guess I'm getting the full mountain experience."

Des laughed. "If that's what you're after, I'll let you shovel the walk in the morning."

Haley's icy blue eyes sparkled with amusement and Des's core heated up. There was that chemistry again, like ice so cold it felt like fire.

"You should take your pants off," she said.

Haley's mouth dropped open, and Des realized what she'd said.

She shook her head. "Not like that." *Unless you want it to be like that.* "You're wearing jeans and they're soaked. You're shivering already." Haley's jaw was trembling, and she seemed to be struggling to control it. Des added, "I'll go see if there's a clean robe in one of the closets for you."

She turned before she gave herself any further excuse to put her foot in her mouth. Just because she thought Haley was the cutest thing on the mountain and she turned Des on every time their eyes met didn't mean Haley wanted to spend the night getting frisky. They were basically trapped in this cabin together until the weather turned, and the last thing Des wanted was to make Haley uncomfortable.

If all they did was light a fire and watch the snow

fall, it'd still be a better night than fighting her way home and then sitting alone in her apartment.

Des found a robe in the closet of the first bedroom she looked in – it appeared housekeeping hadn't made it out to this cabin yet, but from the pristine press of the robe, she could tell it hadn't been used. When she returned to the living room, robe draped over her arm, Haley was standing right where she'd left her, but now she was pantsless, and she'd shed her big red coat and her snow boots too.

Des's first instinct was to look away and apologize... but then she caught the challenging look in Haley's eyes, and the sultry way she laid one hand on her hip.

This was intentional.

Des took a longer look. Haley wore an oversized knit sweater, draped alluringly over the swells of her breasts. Her thighs were creamy and thick, enough for Des to sink her fingers into as she buried her face between them... god, she was practically drooling. And she hadn't said a word since stepping back into the room.

She took a few steps closer. "I found a robe, but it looks like you don't want it just yet."

Haley stepped closer too – now there was barely a foot between them, and Des became aware of how wet her own clothes were. She was dressed for the weather so none of the moisture had seeped through, but she couldn't touch Haley's warm, dry skin dressed like this. All the more reason to strip down to match her. If that was really what she wanted.

"Are you cold?" Des asked.

"A little," Haley answered. "Want to come sit by the fireplace with me?"

Des nodded, and Haley walked over to the gas fireplace situated at an angle in one corner of the living room, the floor-to-ceiling windows right beside it. There was a great view out there, when the snow wasn't obliterating the mountains, but Des wasn't looking outside. She was watching the way Haley's deliciously curvy hips swayed while she walked, and drinking in the sight of her plump cheeks poking out of the bottoms of her panties.

God damn, how did Cupid know exactly what type of woman to send her this Valentine's Day? And it was only February second, to boot.

Haley lit the fireplace with the flick of a switch, then turned to her. "You coming?"

Des didn't waste any time in crossing the room, losing wet outer layers as she went. By the time she reached Haley, she was in the thermal shirt and fleece-lined leggings she wore beneath her work clothes, and she didn't leave any distance between them, either. She walked right up to Haley and took her in her arms, tucking a loose strand of blonde hair out of her face and claiming her mouth with her own.

Haley melted in her arms. She was a few inches shorter than Des and had to tilt her face up to meet her lips. She looked even tastier in the soft light from the gas fireplace, and Des couldn't wait to devour every inch of her.

5
HALEY

This is so not you. You do not just hook up with women you met yesterday! Who even is this woman?

A constant stream of doubt ran through Haley's head, speaking the truth but also distracting her from the hottest kiss she could remember having. Maybe the hottest one she'd ever had.

Des had her arms wrapped around Haley's waist, their bodies pressed together like puzzle pieces, like lovers who knew every dip and curve of each other's bodies, not like strangers who'd just met. Her tongue was exploring Haley's mouth and lighting a fire in her core that threatened to rage out of control, and the scent of her cologne, rich and woodsy, with just a hint of lavender, made Haley dizzy in a way she craved.

Shut up, she told all her doubts. *You don't define me. I'm doing this.*

I'm fucking enjoying this.

Her hands went to Des's body, tentatively brushing over her lower back, then more boldly exploring the curves of her ass. Des groaned encouragement against Haley's lips, then squeezed Haley's ass in return. The move brought their hips tighter against each other, stoking the fire building within her.

The next thing she knew, Haley was pulling Des's shirt over her head, casting it aside. This was so not like her, to take what she craved and think of nothing else but the present moment… but she loved it.

She closed her eyes when Des lifted her sweater over her head, then reached behind her back to unclasp her bra. The whisper of her fingertips over her skin, her warm breath tickling her neck as she did it was sublime. Haley couldn't wait to get this woman naked and feel Des's full form pressed against her own.

They took turns stripping each other bare, turning it into a game of its own rather than a mere necessity to get to the next part. Des let her eyes linger over every inch of Haley's body as it was exposed, an appreciative, hungry smile on her lips that Haley could have spent the rest of her life enjoying.

Then at last, stark naked and without a shred of self-consciousness, Des walked over to the couch nearby and retrieved a lap blanket, as well as a couple of throw pillows. She arranged them on the floor in front of the fire, just close enough to benefit from the heat it was giving off.

Not that Haley particularly needed it in that moment – she was bringing heat of her own.

Des held out her hand and Haley took it, letting her pull her down onto the soft fleece. Des lay her down, Haley's head coming to rest on one of the pillows, with Des's knee between her thighs. Their breasts pressed together as Des leaned over Haley to kiss her and run her hand through her hair again.

"You're gorgeous," she said. "I could tell even from twelve feet above you. I like you so much better right here below me, though."

Her voice was velvety and seductive, and a tiny jolt of displeasure shot into Haley's belly. She was so smooth, Haley got the impression that she wasn't the first woman to succumb to Des's seductions here on the mountain. How many women had Des said that exact line to before her?

She shoved it aside. It didn't matter – Des was hers right now, and Haley couldn't deny the earnestness of the way Des looked at her. Like she really was gorgeous, like there was nowhere she'd rather be.

"I like it too," she said, tilting her hip up to meet Des's thigh.

Des pressed more firmly against her. She kissed Haley again, then started working her way down, along her jaw and slowly down the slope of her neck. Haley closed her eyes, once more losing herself to the moment. When she felt Des nudge her thighs wider and settle between them, her breath hot against Haley's clit, she arched her back and opened her eyes to the sight of snow falling hard just outside the massive windows.

She couldn't see the mountains, or even the landscaping just outside the cabin. The whole world beyond that glass was a wall of white flurries. It didn't matter, though. The only thing she cared about right now was Des's tongue lapping her clit, venturing down between her folds. The warmth of the fireplace. The safety of the cabin.

Des's fingers sliding through her wetness and then pressing into her.

"Oh God," she gasped, hands fisting around the fleece throw.

Neither of them had bothered to turn a light on when they first got to the cabin, and now it was fully dark outside, the snowstorm raging on. The only light within the cabin came from the fireplace, but that suited Haley just fine.

She and Des were still on the floor in front of it, wrapped up in the blanket with their feet poking out to be warmed by the fire. Haley was lying in the crook of Des's arm, her head resting on her shoulder, Des's head on a pillow. Every once in a while, Des ran a hand through Haley's hair, tucking a strand behind her ear or just twirling a lock around her finger. Haley felt silly thinking it, but that feeling of being doted on and fussed over was maybe better than the sex.

Which had been hot as hell – maybe the best she'd ever had.

But just lying like this after, watching the snow fall and listening to Des's heartbeat… it felt special.

"Thanks for rescuing me from the blizzard, by the way," she said after a long, peaceful silence. "It came on fast."

"I'm glad I spotted you – that red coat might have saved your life," Des said. "What were you doing out there, anyway? Didn't you get the thousand alerts Greg sent to all the guests?"

"I did," Haley said. "I guess I'm that one dumbass who thinks the locals are overreacting."

Des snorted. "There is always one."

"I was out taking pictures – trying to catch what Golden Hour light I could in spite of the clouds," she said. "And I was on my way back to the cabin, but I guess not fast enough."

She tilted her head up to look at Des, trying to read her face and discern just how stupid she'd been, walking around instead of going back to the cabin with Val–

Haley sat bolt upright. "Oh my God, Val."

"What?" Des sat up too.

"My friend, I'm here with her," Haley explained, getting up and looking for her coat where she'd discarded it near the door. "I forgot all about her and it's been storming hard for an hour. She must think I'm lost and frozen solid by now. Shit!"

She found her phone, and tapped Val's number. She rarely called, but this didn't seem like a good time for a text.

"Haley, where are you?" Val answered. "Are you okay?"

"I'm fine, I'm so sorry," Haley said. She'd told Val she was going to photograph the ski slopes, and that she'd be right back. They were going to try their hand at cooking in the cabin kitchen since everyone had been warned to stay in their accommodations until the storm passed. "I'm in cabin twenty."

"Umm, you crashed someone else's cabin?"

"No, I'm..." She looked at Des, who was unapologetically listening in on the conversation. There was a glimmer in her eye as she waited for Haley's explanation with as much anticipation as Val. "It was empty. I'm here with one of the resort staff. I'll explain later."

How, exactly, she wasn't sure... but she'd cross that bridge when she came to it.

"I don't think we can leave now," Haley said, glancing out the window. "Are you okay on your own for the night?"

"Do I have a choice?" Val asked.

"Sorry," Haley said. "I'll come back as soon as I can."

"Okay," Val answered. "I'll call off the search party."

"Seriously? A search party?"

"Haley, there's a freaking blizzard and you didn't come back!"

"I can use my walkie-talkie," Des cut in. "I'll let them know you're safe and sound."

Haley breathed a sigh of relief. "Des says she'll tell the resort I'm okay."

"Des?"

Shit. Haley could practically feel Val smiling through the phone.

"This wouldn't happen to be the 'somebody' that you met the other day?"

"Val, I have to go," she said.

"Bullshit, we're snowed in," Val shot back without missing a beat. "Where do you have to be?"

"Stay warm, okay? I'll see you in the morning, or whenever this storm passes."

"Oh, with Des, that's where you need to be," Val said. Yeah, she was definitely grinning like an idiot right now. And Haley was having trouble keeping a smile off her own face.

"Night, Val."

"Night, Haley," Val answered. Just before Haley hung up, she added, "Keep an open mind."

Haley hung up to find Des looking at her camera sitting on the entry table. She'd capped the lens and tucked the bulky equipment into her coat when the snow started falling hard, and it looked like it was no worse for the wear. Des looked up at her, a smirk on her lips.

"I've just put two and two together," she said. "You're the ones from *Traverse,* you and your friend Val. Right?"

Haley nodded. "Don't worry – I'm just the photographer. None of what just happened will make it into the article."

"I imagine that'd be a story for a different kind of magazine," Des said with a wink. "I better contact the lodge *tout de suite* – Greg probably has the whole staff out looking for you."

"Oh God, I hope not," Haley said, her cheeks heating up. "Can you make it sound like I was stuck in the storm for some reason other than my own hubris?"

"Hubris, big word," Des said. "Are you sure you're not a writer?"

"You're the one casually tossing out French phrases," Haley shot back with a smile.

Des retrieved her walkie from her coveralls and smoothed everything over, letting the night manager know Haley would be staying safe and sound with her in cabin twenty until the storm passed. As soon as Haley was sure her face wasn't in imminent danger of appearing on a milk carton, she put her sweater and panties back on and wandered into the kitchen.

It was large and well-appointed with shiny stainless appliances, but other than some cookware, all the cupboards were empty. She found a pair of cellophane-wrapped, heart-shaped cookies on the counter, iced with the resort's logo. But that was the extent of the food.

Des came over, wearing her leggings and the sports bra she'd had on under her thermal shirt. She wrapped her arms around Haley's waist from behind and rested her chin on Haley's shoulder. "Hungry?"

"Getting there," Haley said, even though her stomach was already growling. "Not sure these are the best nourishment for being snowed in."

"The previous guests must have left them," Des said. "Housekeeping sets them out for all the Valentine's bookings."

"Val and I got mascarpone-stuffed strawberries."

"That's cuz Greg is a suck-up."

Haley twisted in her arms, squeezing Des's hips as another wave of desire worked its way through her. "I like your brand of sucking better."

She met Des's eyes, dark brown, nearly black and yet the warmest, most mesmerizing eyes she'd ever seen. And that colorful hair, short and swept back messily after their roll in front of the fireplace... Haley wanted to run her fingers through it, feel the shorn sides of Des's head. Hell, they had all night.

"That thing you did with my leg over your shoulder..."

"What about it?" Des asked.

"I liked it."

Des grinned. "Is that all? Just 'liked'? I must not have been doing it right, then."

"Oh really?"

Des abruptly tightened her arms around Haley's waist, lifting her onto the counter. "Yeah, but I'm not a quitter. Let me try it again."

She peeled Haley's panties away and then dropped to her knees, nudging both of Haley's legs over her shoulders as she pulled her to the edge of the counter.

Haley dropped the cookies, every last thought of food leaving her mind as a new kind of hunger took over.

The two of them never strayed far from the fireplace through the night. The cabin was heated to a comfortable level, but there was something irresistible about snuggling up in front of those big windows, the fireplace giving off a soft, warm glow.

They did eventually leave the floor in favor of the large, comfy couch with an oversized ottoman to stretch their legs on. And when the cookies had been devoured – just as they'd greedily devoured each other – Haley's eyelids began to grow heavy with exhaustion. She fell asleep in Des's arms, body curled up against her, inhaling the musky richness of her cologne with every breath.

And in the morning, she woke up alone.

Her very first realization on opening her eyes was that the blizzard had ended, leaving the whole mountain blanketed in a deep layer of fresh snow – far too bright for first thing in the morning.

She squinted and turned away from the window, intent on burying her face against Des's soft skin. And that's when she noticed she was alone on the couch. The fleece throw had been carefully tucked around her and she had a pillow under her head instead of Des's arm.

She must be in the bathroom, Haley thought, but when she sat up and looked around, the cabin was utterly silent. Des had turned the flame of the fireplace down low, and none of her clothes were where she'd left them on the floor the night before. Even her boots were gone.

"Des?" Haley called out, already knowing she would be met with silence.

She wrapped the blanket around her shoulders and stood, noticing that Des had taken the time to lay her jeans over the back of one of the dining chairs so they'd dry. Beside them were the rest of Haley's clothes in a neat little pile, and on top of that, a note. Haley let out a sigh as she crossed the room to read it.

Had to report to work, didn't want to wake you. Thank you for a lovely evening – one of the best I've had since I started here. Hope you enjoyed yourself too, and if you did I expect a mention in your Yelp review, if not the magazine article.

Des

PS – Please lock the door on your way out, wouldn't want delinquents getting in and doing unspeakable things by the fire ;)

She read through it twice, feeling like she'd just been sideswiped by a bus. Des couldn't take the time to wake her up and say all this in person, but she did have the time to tidy up before she left? Bullshit. She just didn't want to endure the awkwardness that came after a one-night stand.

And that was all Haley was to her. That was the part that hurt, because against all odds, against her better judgment, last night she'd allowed herself to believe there was real chemistry between them.

Haley wasn't naïve, she knew sleeping with someone she met on assignment, someone who lived a thousand miles away, wouldn't lead to a long-term relationship. What they were doing last night wasn't the start of a happily ever after. She didn't even want that.

But she thought she meant more to Des than this Dear Jane note.

She crumpled it and swallowed the lump that was forming in her throat. The worst part was that she knew going in that this would be nothing but meaningless sex. And she *still* managed to develop feelings for Des in the space of a single night.

Feelings she had no right to have.

Feelings she couldn't expect Des to anticipate.

Feelings she should dispense with as quickly as possible for her own good. How the hell had this happened?

Incredibly hot sex in a ridiculously romantic loca-

tion? How could it not? that little devil's advocate in her mind shot back.

"Well, I'm here to do a job," Haley said aloud. "This was a fun little diversion… but now it's back to work."

That was exactly what Des's note had said, wasn't it? Haley threw it away then got dressed and turned off the fireplace. She put on her coat and boots, now pleasantly dry and warm, and flipped up her hood. Then at the last minute, she went to the kitchen trash and took the crumpled note out of it, stuffing it in her coat pocket. The only thing worse than confusing a one-night stand for something meaningful would be letting the housekeeping staff read all about it.

6

DES

*D*es got to the lodge a few minutes early for her shift. The brightness of the fresh-fallen snow had woken her at the crack of dawn, which was lucky because she'd been so wrapped up in Haley that she forgot to set an alarm.

Part of her had hoped the blizzard would last forever, or at least through the day. How could Greg expect her to show up for work in white-out conditions? But the storm had passed in the night, and when she woke up she knew it would be best if she got her butt into gear and showed up a little early. He'd have questions for her, and the sooner she answered them, the sooner she could get to the coffee maker in the break room.

Maybe steal a muffin off the continental breakfast buffet too, she was thinking as she headed for the timeclock. She was surprisingly energetic, probably because what she wrote in her note to Haley was true – last night had been amazing.

Fucking mind-blowing, actually, but she'd toned it down so as not to come off too intensely.

Des was no worse for the lack of sleep – at least so far – but she sure could use some food. One Valentine's-themed sugar cookie did not a dinner make.

No sooner had her finger touched the screen of the timeclock, however, than she heard her full name. She tried not to visibly raise her hackles.

"Destiny, can I see you in my office?" Greg asked from the doorway behind her. She tried to read his tone – pissed off that she'd spent the night in a luxury cabin that still needed to be cleaned and patched before the next guests arrived? Annoyed that she'd waited so long to fix the roof? One thing was for sure, she didn't hear a whole lot of gratitude for rescuing the resort's MVG – Most Valuable Guest.

"Sure thing, boss," she said. "One sec."

"Now," Greg answered. "I have to adjust your timecard manually anyway, since you never clocked out last night."

"Right." Des turned to follow him down the hall to his office, like a scolded puppy. "Sorry about that. Did you get home safely?"

A little sucking up never hurt, and hell, she'd been

working with the guy for nearly six months now. It was impossible not to care about your coworkers at least a little, even if they were micromanaging, meddling and obnoxiously enthusiastic.

"Yes, I left a little early yesterday to drive Ivan home," he said. "I don't quite trust him behind the wheel in snow like that – he doesn't have enough experience yet."

"He's lucky to have you," Des said. She hardly knew her own relatives beyond the immediate family – they lived all over the country and growing up, it had just been her and her parents in Emerald Hill.

"Have a seat," Greg said as they stepped into his office. It was nice, but cluttered. There were papers all over his desk and a huge year-long calendar pinned to one wall, outlining every event the resort had planned and everything Greg needed to do to pull them all off.

Des sat in an upholstered chair across from his desk, and Greg sat in his well-worn office chair.

"The night manager filled me in on everything," he said.

Des decided the best strategy was to get out in front of whatever he was planning to complain about. "Greg, I'm sorry about last night – the storm snuck up on me, and I had no choice. I left the cabin as neat as I could–"

He waved her explanation away. "It happens."

Des arched an eyebrow. "Really?"

"Destiny, you've been living in this area your whole life, right?" She nodded. "Then you know as well as I do that these winter storms can be unpredictable. You took shelter, and more importantly, you prioritized a guest's safety. I'm proud of you for that."

Des frowned. Why had she been pulled into the boss's office, then, if he was *proud* of her? Greg wasn't the type to have a sit-down chat just to dole out accolades. "I'm sorry, what's the problem, then?"

Greg leaned forward, forearms resting on his desk. "Protocol."

"Protocol?"

"You saved the day yesterday, and I'm going to make sure everyone knows about it," he said. Des bit back the urge to say *I'd rather you didn't*. "But the fact remains that you made several very dangerous decisions. One, working on a roof in inclement weather all by yourself – you could have fallen and broken your neck, and we'd just now be finding you in a snow drift. Two, why on earth didn't you radio the lodge right away when you rescued Ms. Thomas from the storm?"

Des averted her gaze, looking out the window beside the desk, never happier that she wasn't the type to blush. "I'm sorry, I didn't realize there were people looking for her." That was true enough, but it wasn't the only reason she'd been distracted in the first hour after taking Haley to cabin twenty.

"You *always* notify the lodge when anything out of the ordinary like that happens," Greg lectured. "Especially in a storm. We could have lost staff as well as the guest if they went out looking for her and got lost."

Oh shit. As uncomfortable as it was to be scolded by the boss, Greg had a point. "The last thing I wanted to do was put anyone in danger. I'm sorry."

Greg sat back in his chair. "I'm going to record the fact that we spoke about this in your personnel file, but I won't consider it a written warning. You are still on probation for a couple more weeks – I want you to succeed here, Destiny. Don't get in your own way."

Struggling against the urge to roll her eyes at that last quip was like trying not to gag once the reflex had been triggered. Greg was a little more than ten years older than her, and he did care a hell of a lot about the resort, but right now he was overstepping. Des just wanted to repair roofs and hang string lights – she didn't need Tony Robbins for a boss.

But he was right – she was on probation, and had practically made a vocation of getting on Greg's bad side. He was extending an olive branch because she'd kept Haley from turning into a photog-cicle, so she gritted her teeth and said, "Thanks for the advice. Is there anything else?"

Greg shook his head. "Get out there and make someone's day."

"Aye-aye, captain." Okay, maybe a little too much sarcasm on that last comment, but Greg didn't seem to notice.

Des got up, thinking she could still make it to the continental breakfast before all the blueberry muffins got snatched up, and when she was alone in the hallway, she chuckled to herself, shaking her head. Would Greg be so nice if he knew *everything* that had happened in cabin twenty last night?

Hell, Haley sure seemed to enjoy herself – maybe he'd give Des a raise for her outstanding customer service.

7
HALEY

When Haley got back to cabin seven, Val immediately asked, "Is Des the woman you were talking about the other day? Did anything happen? Give me details!"

Haley clammed up, embarrassment choking her. The insult of that horribly impersonal note was too fresh, and she felt foolish for letting herself expect more. She reassured Val that she was safe through the storm and apologized for worrying her, and then she redirected her best friend's attention to a subject she knew would distract her – food.

"I don't know about you, but I'm starving," she said. "There were a couple of cookies in the cabin, and we were lucky to even have that."

"Well, I got bored without you here and got into

the champagne," Val said. "Ended up drinking half the bottle."

"Sounds like you could use some greasy hangover food," Haley said.

So they made their way to the lodge for breakfast, impressed by the speed with which the resort staff had plowed the streets and shoveled the walkways. Then, because the first Valentine's-related event – speed dating for the singles – wasn't scheduled until the evening, they decided to make the most of the fresh powder.

They rented skis and Haley gave Val a quick lesson in the basics – how to snowplow in order to stop, the best way to get on the ski lift, how to walk in cumbersome, inflexible ski boots. She was no expert herself, but she'd skied a few times, and she would have tackled the moguls in Telluride if it meant forgetting Des and that damn note. Trying not to die or break something on the challenging slopes of Emerald Mountain thankfully provided that opportunity.

And Val was a quick study. She'd never skied before, but she did know how to ice skate so the balance element of the sport was simple for her to pick up. Too simple, apparently, because before long she was pestering Haley about her night.

"I really don't want to talk about it," Haley told her on the ski lift.

"But *why*?" Val asked. "I mean, I was *so bored* by myself last night – the storm knocked out my cell reception so I couldn't call Moska, and even the TV was fuzzy thanks to all the snow on the satellite dishes. I just wanna know what you and *Des* did to pass the time."

Haley's cheeks colored and Val noticed it instantly. That wasn't her journalistic training – that was a best friend's instinct.

"I knew it! You slept with her!"

"Fine, yes!" Haley admitted with a huff. It was only ten a.m. and Haley sensed that Val wouldn't stop at anything short of 'enhanced interrogation techniques' to get this gossip out of her. As much as Haley wanted to put it behind her, it was better to just give Val what she wanted.

"Well?" Val prompted. "How was it?"

Haley let out a sigh. If she was going to talk, she might as well get it all out. "It was fucking amazing."

Val squealed. "Really?"

"We laid on a blanket in front of the fire just like in sappy movies, and it really was super romantic," she said. "And not to be crude–"

"Oh please, be crude," Val encouraged.

"I'm actually *sore* this morning – that's how much sex we had, like horny little bunnies."

"Snow bunnies," Val interjected, then arched an eyebrow. "Wait, is that a new experience for you? Fucking yourself raw?"

Haley snorted. If she'd been drinking, it would have been a spit take. "I mean... yeah?"

"Good lord, you have been missing out," Val said. "How are you five years older than me?" She looked up at the sky, clear and perfectly light blue as if the storm of the century hadn't blown through last night. "This girl needs someone who knows how to fuck her right!"

"Val!" Haley said, scrunching down in her coat. "Voices carry out here."

"Who cares?" Val asked. "Don't *you* feel like shouting this morning, after all that great sex?"

Kind of, Haley thought. She had when she first woke up, before she realized Des wasn't at her side anymore. "Here comes the drop-off."

She counted down for Val's sake, and they both hopped off the lift. Haley pulled her friend out of the way so the people in the chair behind them would have a wide-open landing spot to do the same, then they waddled awkwardly over to the top of the slope in their skis. It was an intermediate slope, because the only beginner hills at the resort were way down by the resort and too tiny to bother with – unless you were taking a lesson or you were under the age of five. And at that, Haley had seen some damn impressive toddlers on skis already today.

"Hey, wait," Val said when she noticed Haley getting ready to push off.

"Huh?"

"You're not going to leave me hanging like that, are you?" she said. "You and Miss 'Fuck Me Til I Can't Walk Straight' are gonna meet up again, right? Hey, you can both sign up for speed dating – that'd be fun!"

"Um, no." There were very few things that sounded like less fun than speed dating, whether Des was involved or not, and Haley was sure Des wouldn't be interested if Haley sat down at her table. She k new the type – the love 'em and leave 'em playgirl. Her ex had been one and look how that had worked out.

"Why not?"

Haley shrugged, mustering every casual fiber in her being – which were not in plentitude. "I think it was just a one-night kind of deal. Circumstances, you know?"

She pushed off with her ski poles before Val had a chance to say anything else, hoping against hope that by the time they got to the bottom of the mountain, she'd have moved on from this topic. Instead, Val cupped her hands around her mouth and shouted after her, "You're not a one-night stand kind of girl, Haley Thomas!"

Oh God, and she had to use her full name, too. Haley cringed, wondering if it would be unforgivable to ditch her loud-mouth friend on an intermediate slope when she barely knew how to ski.

She was tempted for a minute or so – about the length of time that Val's shout echoed through the air. And then she took a wide turn to her right, looking over her shoulder for her friend. Val was behind her, doing her best to keep up with more courage than skill, and Haley slowed down so they could go down the mountain together.

Val was right, after all. Last night was the first one-night stand Haley had ever had, and given how it ended, she was in no rush to have another.

"This is beautiful!" Val shouted over the wind. "Did you bring your camera?"

"No way," Haley said. "My luck, I'd wipe out and land on it."

"We should ask the manager to drive us up here in a snowmobile later, then," she said. "You'd get some beautiful shots – maybe even a cover photo."

In the two years she'd been working for *Traverse,* Haley had been a rising star. Even stodgy old Art had to acknowledge the good work she did. But she'd never gotten a cover shot – not yet. But hell, she was doing a lot of things she'd never done before on this trip. Maybe it was in the cards for her.

Des, though? As wishful and optimistic as Val liked to be, Haley was the one who'd read the note.

And she knew whatever spark they'd had burned out this morning when Des woke up next to her and decided to sneak out of the cabin without saying goodbye.

8
DES

*D*es kept an eye out for Haley as she went about her work, expecting to see her out taking pictures or maybe even wandering around the resort, looking for her?

When she didn't bump into her at all on the day after their adventure in cabin twenty, Des briefly considered popping by cabin seven to say hello. Maybe bring Haley some more of the mascarpone-stuffed strawberries she'd raved about in the middle of the night when the cookies were long gone and both their stomachs had been rumbling.

But she had a long to-do list from Greg, and that seemed too forward for her, anyway. When was the last time she'd pursued a woman like that? Or even wanted to see her again after she'd bedded her? That part of Des's heart had been closed off for years, and she knew from experience how badly it hurt to go there. The last time, she'd damn near been mortally wounded.

Haley was fun. She put a smile on Des's face and her body was fucking incredible, especially when it was pressed up against Des's with not a scrap of fabric between them. But it was probably best for everyone if Des didn't let herself get too enamored. That was why she decided not to look too hard for her. She went about her day, letting Haley decide whether to come find her.

Greg came to Des early in her shift the next day, looking on the verge of a breakdown. "Are you busy this evening, Destiny?"

"Why, are you asking me to the dance?"

She should have known it wasn't the time to tease him. He'd been pulling his hair out for months over the Valentine's extravaganza that was going to put Emerald Mountain Ski Resort on the romantic destination map, and since the snowstorm it had been all hands on deck. But Greg was so easy to frazzle, who could resist a little teasing?

"In a manner of speaking, actually, yes," he surprised her. "Two of my event staff are still snowed in from the storm, and Ivan volunteered to stay late to assist during tonight's dance lesson, but he's got a terrible head cold and I don't want him around the guests while he's contagious."

"Are you offering me overtime?" Des asked.

Greg looked at her like he hadn't been planning to, but considering how few options he had, he relented. And Des happily accepted.

So that was how she came to be standing behind the refreshment table, wearing a button-down white shirt and a bowtie, watching two dozen couples awkwardly follow the instructions of a ballroom dance teacher.

The guests at this event skewed older, many of them with silver streaks in their hair and orthopedics in their shoes, trying to rekindle the flames of mature relationships through the magic of the foxtrot. Something squeezed in Des's chest watching them, forcing her to imagine herself with the same woman for twenty, thirty, forty years.

Once upon a time, she'd thought that was in the cards for her.

"Pardon me," a woman in a full, sweeping skirt got her attention. She pointed to the restroom. "The toilet paper is running low in there."

"No problem, I'll refill it," Des said.

The woman rejoined her partner on the dance floor and Des did her janitorial duties. When she emerged from the restroom, the dance instructor had borrowed someone's husband to demonstrate the steps of a waltz. Everyone else was sitting down at the tables arranged around the perimeter of the dance floor, paying close attention.

Everyone except a certain icy-eyed beauty, who must have arrived while Des was restocking toilet paper. Haley was removing her coat, and their eyes locked from across the room. She wore a red velvet dress that swished at her hips when she moved, and Des couldn't resist following the curves of her legs in silky-looking tights down to a pair of incongruous snow boots. She looked just as hot now as she had when Des came out of the bedroom of cabin twenty and found her wearing only her sweater and a pair of panties.

That had put her heart right in her throat and turned her on like nothing else.

Haley looked away from her now, though, taking a seat and speaking to a dark-haired woman who was scribbling notes on a steno pad. Des guessed that must be Val, the best-friend-slash-journalist. Before she could decide whether to go say hello – would that be awkward? – the dance instructor called her to the front of the room.

"I thought I had my music all queued up in the right order," she explained when Des met her by the AV cabinet. "But this next song isn't for waltzing, it's for the rumba."

"I'll figure it out," Des promised. "Can I see your phone?"

The instructor handed it over and Des flicked through the playlist and the woman told her the name of the song she wanted. "I teach lessons all over the state and I love it," she was saying, "but the technology is going to be the death of me. The setup is never the same in any two places."

Des tapped the play button and the instructor's eyes lit up.

"That's it, you're a genius!"

Just a digital native, Des thought, then handed the woman her phone. "Happy to help."

"Okay, everyone, partner up and find a place on the dance floor!" she called. "I'll circulate to help you out."

The room was chaos then, and Des lost her opportunity to go say hello to Haley. Instead, she made her way back to the refreshment table, eyeing the punch bowl and the Linzer cookies with little hearts cut out of their centers, making sure the supplies didn't dip too low.

For the first few minutes of the waltz, the room was filled with couples awkwardly bumping into each other, clumsily stepping on their partners' toes. The instructor made corrections here and there, and soon the majority of them were dancing along smoothly.

Technology might not be her forte, but the woman was good at her job.

Then Des glanced back at Haley's table and was surprised to find her still sitting there. Val was hunched over her notebook, looking entirely absorbed in writing about the event, and Haley had her camera out, but even across the room, Des could see the look of longing in her eyes. She didn't want to be looking at other dancers through a lens. She wanted to be out there herself.

Greg would lose his shit if he knew Des was getting paid overtime to invite pretty ladies to dance, but Greg wasn't here. He'd left at his usual time and was probably at home now, being an overbearing terror to his wife and kids. So Des skirted around the refreshment table and went to Haley.

"Hi."

Haley looked a little surprised, her eyes sweeping over Des's formalwear. Then her face became unreadable, like a mask. "Hey."

Her friend looked up from her notebook at last. "Is this...?"

Haley looked pained. "Yes. This is Des. Des, Val. She's my better half when it comes to the magazine."

An unexpected bolt of jealousy struck Des in the belly at Haley's choice of words. She'd just met her, but already she felt possessive, and the idea of her having a better half who wasn't Des was indigestible. Silly, too, of course.

Des held out her hand. "It's nice to meet you, Val. Haley told me all about your adventures together."

Val shook her hand, but there was a playful glimmer in her eyes. "I'm surprised you two had time to talk."

Des's mouth fell open slightly, as did Haley's.

"Val!"

"Oh come on, it's nothing to be embarrassed about," she went on. "If Moska was here with all this romantic ambiance, we sure as hell wouldn't be doing much talking."

"Okay, that's enough from you," Haley said, tapping Val's notebook. "Don't you have notes to take?"

Val chuckled, but she diverted her attention just like Haley wanted. Or at least pretended to – Des was pretty sure she was still listening in.

Des held her hand out to Haley. "Would you care to dance?"

She frowned. "I'm really only here to take pictures."

"And I'm here to fill the punch bowl," Des pointed out. "I won't tell if you don't."

"Go for it," Val interjected, not looking up from her notebook.

There was something more than just a sense of

duty holding Haley back, though. Des could feel an invisible wall between them that hadn't been there before – not even the first day they met, when Haley was looking up at Des on that archway, not bothering to disguise the desire in her eyes.

Then the dance instructor came by and lifted Haley's hand, placing it in Des's outstretched palm. "Go on, dear, you'll learn so much more from experience than you will sitting on the sidelines."

And then she was gone, and Haley had no choice but to accept Des's offer. She stood, set her camera on the table, and allowed Des to lead her to an open spot on the dance floor. Haley was still wearing her boots, which Des found irrationally charming. And the feel of soft velvet where Des's hand came to rest at the small of Haley's back made her want to do so much more than waltz with her.

"Were you paying attention to the steps?" she asked.

Haley shook her head. "Let's just do what they're doing?" She nodded to the nearest couple, who seemed to have it down.

"I'll lead," Des said. Never mind the fact that she had no idea what she was doing. She straightened her back, held her head high and substituted confidence for knowledge. "Back, right, left..."

Now they were the ones stepping on each other's

toes, their bodies colliding when Des stepped forward and Haley did too, narrowly avoiding other couples on the dance floor. Des was smiling at their clumsiness, but all of Haley's playfulness from their night together was gone. She was looking at their feet, a stern expression furrowing her brow, determined to get it right.

"Look at your partner, dear," the dance instructor said, stepping in to fix the disaster.

She put one finger under Haley's chin, lifting it until her eyes locked with Des's. There was a spark in them, but it wasn't the same smoldering one Des loved from before. This one almost looked like anger. Was she so competitive that not immediately nailing the waltz was pissing her off?

"Okay, let's get this box step under control," the instructor said. She did just that in a matter of seconds – pretty impressive considering where Des and Haley had started. She left them competently waltzing, if a tad mechanically.

"I think we've got it," Des said with a grin.

"Guess you can check it off your list, then," Haley shot back, her words so sharp they stung.

"What?"

The song ended and Des prayed that the instructor wouldn't need her help again. She didn't want to let Haley out of her arms, especially when she was staring daggers at her. But Haley broke free anyway, grumbling, "Thanks for the dance."

"Okay, everyone, good waltzing," the instructor said. "Next up, I'm going to show you the tango..."

Des was barely listening to her. She watched Haley go back to her table, say something to Val, then snatch her coat and camera and head out the door. Des looked at Val, bewildered, unsurprised to see Val giving her a dirty look. Des had no idea what she'd done, but her stomach turned to stone and her heart was tightening in her chest.

Why should I care why a stranger is mad at me? she tried to tell herself. But she did – whether she wanted to or not, she cared.

9
HALEY

What the hell was Des doing? First she literally wrote Haley off, and now she was flirting with her and making her *feel things* all over again on the dance floor?

Des might be the type of person who could have completely meaningless sex and seduce women she didn't care about, but Haley wasn't. As much as she'd tried.

As she stomped through the snow to the main lodge, her camera swinging at her side, it occurred to her that she shouldn't be mad at Des. She was the one who took Val's stupid advice to cut loose and see where it took her.

And yet...

She *was* mad at Des.

If all she wanted was a hookup, and to casually flirt

with Haley on the dance floor, she never should have seduced her with those burning chestnut eyes. She shouldn't have delicately wrapped Haley up in a blanket after they were done having sex, making sure she was warm and cozy and falling asleep in her arms. She shouldn't have acted like she cared so damn much!

Haley didn't even notice that her coat was slung over her arm rather than wrapped around her until she was more than halfway to the lodge. The cold belatedly bit into her, but there didn't seem much point in putting it on now. She trudged the last few feet and hung her coat on a rack by the door, then made a bee line for the bar in the lounge area.

There were about a dozen guests there, mostly coupled up, apparently disinterested in learning to foxtrot. Haley ignored them as she slid onto a barstool and a bartender in a bowtie came over. He was wearing the same uniform Des had on tonight, and Haley thought grumpily that it looked much better on Des. There wasn't much that beat a woman in dress pants, although she'd been pretty damn turned on by Des in her coveralls too.

Why'd she have to be so freaking hot?

"What'll it be, miss?" the bartender asked, setting a napkin down in front of her.

Haley considered for a moment. Booze would only make her problems worse, and she had to be up early tomorrow morning for couples' yoga. Besides, she was still shivering from walking through the snow in only her dress and her boots. She needed something warm.

"Hot cocoa?"

"Coming right up," the bartender said.

He disappeared into a little prep area behind the bar, and Haley swiveled in her seat to take in the room. There was a fireplace at one end with real logs crackling within it, and as she'd come to expect, huge windows with spectacular views of the mountain. It was dark now, so there wasn't much to see out there. Inside, the couples around her were absorbed in each other, either snuggled up together in loveseats or sipping drinks and giving each other googly eyes.

"Here you are," the bartender said, and Haley turned back around to find a red mug with little pink, heart-shaped marshmallows floating in her cocoa. Damn it, even the beverages were romantic here. The resort was doing a bang-up job with its Valentine's theme, great new for everybody who came here looking for that.

A little bit sickening for Haley at the moment. *Ten more days*.

"Can I have a spoon, please?" she asked the bartender as she set her camera on the bar top and settled in.

He gave her one, then headed down to the other

end of the bar to refill a couple's drinks. Haley was busy drowning her heart-shaped marshmallows when she heard someone else's voice at her side. "Haley?"

It was soft and velvety, and her heart started to climb into her throat. She turned to see Des standing there, also sans coat, her cheeks rosy from the wind.

"Do you mind if I sit?" she asked.

Haley gave a dispassionate shrug. *It's a free country,* she nearly said, but bit back the words. She was hurt, but she wasn't twelve.

Des sat on the stool beside her and waved the bartender off when he came to take her order. She only had eyes for Haley, her whole body turned toward her. And that was exactly the kind of mixed signal that was driving Haley so crazy!

"Did I do something wrong?" Des asked.

Haley glanced at her. Des's eyes were big and glassy like a puppy dog's, like she genuinely had no clue why her conquest might be feeling upset after Des ghosted her. Haley set her jaw and lifted her spoon from her mug. The marshmallows hadn't fully melted but they were no longer recognizable as hearts. She set the spoon down on her napkin and took a slow drink, hoping Des would just give up and walk away, just like so many other women in her life had.

The hot cocoa was some of the best she'd ever

tasted – almost better than that mascarpone-stuffed strawberry. Dammit, this resort did food well.

Des was still sitting there patiently when Haley lowered her mug. Okay, so they were doing this. She swiveled her stool to face her, careful not to let their knees touch. Haley wasn't about to start sending her own confusing signals. She fidgeted with her nails, idly picking at her gel polish even though she knew it would damage the nailbeds.

"Do you seriously not know?" she asked.

Des's brow furrowed. "I had a really good time with you the other night."

Haley snorted. That was exactly what her note had said. "Is that why you vanished the next morning? Honestly, no note at all would have been kinder."

She ripped a big strip of gel polish off and grimaced at the damage she was doing. Then Des put her hand on top of Haley's, stopping her fidgeting. There was genuine confusion in her eyes as she asked, "What was wrong with my note?"

Haley's eyes narrowed when she asked, "Felt an awful lot like a form letter to me. Is that the exact wording you use for every woman you sleep with?"

Des's mouth dropped open and Haley had to admit her shock looked genuine. She already felt bad for her harsh words, but there was no going back.

"Okay, look, I'm not used to the whole one-night

stand thing, but I get the impression that you're no stranger to it," she hurried on, the words coming out in a torrent. "I thought we had a real connection and so I was really surprised and a bit hurt when I woke up to find you gone without even saying goodbye." *God, kill me now,* she thought, but everything that had been building in her for the last couple of days just kept pouring out. "It's fine, I'll get over it, but I'm not the kind of person that can just sleep around casually without it meaning anything, so I don't think it's a good idea for us to–"

"Haley?" Des squeezed her hand and Haley stopped talking long enough to look at her.

She'd been fully prepared to hate Des, to radiate anger in her direction until she gave up and went away. But there was real concern etched on her face now, and Haley had the urge to hear Des out.

"What?"

"I'm sorry I didn't wake you up," she said. "I had to leave really early because I haven't really been on my boss's good side in a while, so I thought I was doing you a favor letting you sleep. I wrote that note really quickly. Was it really that bad?"

Haley went over to the coatrack and retrieved it from the pocket of her coat. She handed it to Des as she sat back down on her stool. While she read, Haley tried to backtrack. She tried to steel her heart and pretend she never felt anything for Des. "We were just stuck in a snowstorm with nothing else to do... you don't owe me anything."

Des looked up from the note. "Okay, I get how you could read this and think I was being flip. I definitely didn't mean it that way."

Haley looked sheepishly at her. "You didn't?"

"Hell no," Des said. "You read me right, casual flings are kind of my go-to, but you were right about the other night too – it's been a really long time since I've had such an instant connection with anyone." She lowered her voice. "And you can't tell me the sex wasn't incredible."

Haley smiled in spite of herself. "It was."

Des scooted her stool a little closer. "I don't want anyone to feel bad because of me, whether we had a fling or not. But if I had to pick a word to describe what happened the other night, it definitely wouldn't be *meaningless.*"

"Really?" Haley's heart was fully in her throat now and she swallowed past the lump. She could smell Des's cologne and she could feel the heat of her body – or maybe that was just the memory of how they felt when they were molded against each other.

"I like you, Haley Thomas," Des answered, then grinned. "And I'm not just saying that because Greg told the whole staff to suck up to you and Val this week."

Haley laughed.

There was that smile again, struggling against Haley's will to stay angry, stay distant. Oh, who was she kidding? Des was looking at her with such earnestness, such desire in those gorgeous eyes, there wasn't a drop of anger left in Haley.

"Why don't we start over?" Des suggested.

"Like, 'hi, my name's Haley, what's yours?'"

Des shook her head. "Nah, we don't have to go that far – it'd be a travesty to pretend the other night never happened. Well, except for this."

She held up the note, then stood up. Haley watched as Des crossed the lounge and crumpled it, tossing it into the fire. When she came back, she dusted off her hands.

"There," she said. "Mistake erased."

Haley finally let herself smile back at Des. "If only all life's problems had such easy solutions."

"Sometimes we just think too hard about them," Des said. "Would you like to go for a walk with me?"

"In the snow?" Haley thought of her tights. Even with her coat on, it had been frigid walking over to the building where the dancing was taking place.

"We'll stay inside where it's warm," Des promised. "I want to show you my favorite place in the lodge."

She held her hand out. Haley frowned at her half-drunk hot cocoa. "I haven't paid for my drink yet."

"They'll charge it to your room," Des said. "Although, if you haven't figured it out yet, you're royalty around here. I wouldn't be surprised if Greg comps you for everything you eat and do while you're here."

Haley laughed. "Well, that'd be dumb of him – we paid with a company credit card so that hot cocoa's not coming out of my pocket."

"In that case, order the grapefruit Bellini," Des said. "It's expensive but delish."

Haley made a mental note of it – Val would definitely want to add that to her notebook. Then she snatched up her camera and coat, and took Des's hand, letting her lead the way. *Keep an open mind.* That's what Val wanted for her. And maybe even an open heart?

10
DES

*D*es didn't release Haley's hand while they walked. It was a calculated risk, considering she was just barely out of the doghouse, but it seemed to be working. Haley even reached over with her free hand to flick Des's bowtie.

"Are you supposed to be working the dance lesson right now?" she asked. "Am I contributing to your bad reputation with Greg?"

"Technically, yes," Des admitted. "But Greg is at home in his comfortable clothes, probably drinking a beer and watching sports in his favorite recliner, or whatever straight men do in the evenings. If he finds out I skipped out on the dance lesson, he won't get to yell at me about it until tomorrow." She squeezed Haley's hand. "That's a risk I'm willing to take."

They passed a couple of night crew staff along the

way, and Des was sure that her attire gave away her AWOL status, but no one batted an eye at that, or the fact that she was holding a guest's hand.

"Where are you taking me?" Haley finally asked when they'd gone down the main hallway, down one floor in the elevator, and were now walking through an employees-only service hall.

"We're almost there," Des promised. There was no one else around at this time of night, and hardly anyone other than the maintenance crew came all the way down here anyway. She pulled her badge out of her pocket and swiped her universal keycard to unlock a door at the end of the hall.

When she pulled it open to reveal a dark, narrow hallway, Haley looked at her dubiously. "You going to murder me down here because we argued?"

Des laughed and reached past the doorframe to turn on a light. "I promise I have no ill intent... maybe sexy intent, if you're lucky."

"They store all kinds of nonsense down here, and I think I've personally hauled up every scrap of Christmas, New Years and Valentine's décor the resort owns," she explained while she led the way down the hall, past a few storage rooms on either side of it. "This part of the building is the original lodge, basically untouched from when it was built in the 20s. Every other space has been renovated and added onto – several times over."

They reached a door at the end of the hallway and this one didn't have an electronic keycard lock. Des turned the knob and pushed the door open. She flipped a light switch within, then stepped aside for Haley.

Haley drew breath beside her. "Oh wow, I wasn't expecting this."

The space was a one-room apartment, with a kitchenette and bathroom and a bed. Every piece of furniture and every single piece of décor was exactly as it had been in the 1920s, and stepping inside was like going through a time warp.

"Me neither," Des said. "I just kinda stumbled on it one day when I was looking for garlands. As far as I can tell, it belonged to the original caretaker and after he retired, the resort chose not to fill his position. Most people would rather commute from Emerald Hill than live 24/7 in the basement of their workplace."

Haley laughed. "My boss would probably love it if I lived 24/7 at the magazine."

"So would mine," Des agreed. "But lucky for me, I'm about ninety percent sure Greg has no idea this room exists – and neither does anybody else, because I'm the only one who ever comes down to this part of the basement. Sometimes I come down here just to breathe for a few minutes when Greg's hassling me."

Haley laughed. "Hiding from your boss... and you say you've gotten on his bad side somehow?"

"Okay, so maybe it's not the biggest mystery in the world," Des said.

Haley made her way further into the room, looking around. The bed was pushed up against the far wall, and there was a rocking chair in the corner by an old wood-burning stove. "Do you mind?" Haley asked, uncapping her camera lens.

"You can't include this room in your article," Des said.

Haley nodded. "I won't ruin your hideout. Can I take a couple pictures for myself?"

Des agreed. She followed Haley around, looking over her shoulder at the viewfinder and trying to see the space through Haley's eyes. "How exactly does this work?" she asked. "Your feature, I mean. Greg said you're staying through Valentine's Day."

"Mm-hmm," Haley answered, only half listening, a stern look of concentration on her face as she visualized her shots. "We're going to cover all the big events. The article will be equal parts written and photo journal."

"And people will care about that after Valentine's Day is over?" Des asked.

Haley looked up at her, brow furrowed, then realized where the disconnect was. "Oh, no. We're doing all this so it's ready to run in February's edition next year." Then she turned her camera lens on Des.

"Oh no, not in the bowtie!" she protested.

Haley chuckled. "Why not? I think it's charming."

"It was this or a dress that resembled something a flight attendant would wear," Des said.

"Well, I'm quite sure you could pull off either, but I like you in the dress pants."

Haley snapped a photo of her, then lowered her camera. Des took a couple steps closer, then ran her hand over Haley's arm, brushing her velvet sleeve smooth. "I like you in this dress. And in your big red coat... and out of it."

Haley bit her lower lip. Her light blue eyes were hot with desire, but she took a step back. "I can't do this."

"What?" Des felt like somebody had dropped that big old wood-burner in the corner into her chest.

"I'm glad we cleared the air and I appreciate you bringing me to your special spot," Haley said. "But I'm no good at casual stuff. I'm only here for ten more days and I like you already. I don't want to get my heart broken."

Des tucked a strand of Haley's hair behind her ear. Raw emotion filled her eyes and made her more beautiful than ever. "What we did the other night was far from meaningless to me."

"Me too," Haley said, her voice barely above a whisper. She looked so scared, so vulnerable, Des just wanted to wrap her up in her arms and never let her go. "Obviously I have no right to ask you for anything–"

"Hey," Des interrupted. "I don't know who in your past gave you the idea that you didn't have a right to ask for what you want, but fuck her and her wrongness."

That earned her a bigger, more authentic smile. It warmed her belly. But there was that whole *leaving in ten days* thing to consider.

"So, what do you want to do?"

Haley's sheepish smile was back. "I have kind of a silly idea."

"I like silly."

"Well, it's Valentine's Day," she said. "Or Valentine's season, at least. And you're single – right?"

Des laughed. "I am."

"And so am I," Haley continued. "And we like each other, but I don't think I could stand it if I knew you were looking at other women too... maybe we can be something more than casual and just enjoy it while it lasts. Until I go home on the fifteenth."

Des considered. She'd only known Haley for a couple days, but it was clear that someone had hurt her, abandoned her. Left a big, old, self-conscious hole in her heart that hurt to touch now. And she wanted to do what she could to help Haley mend that wound, make her whole again. If a serious-but-temporary arrangement would help...

But that didn't mean her own heart was unbreakable. There were hairline cracks all through it, just waiting to shatter. And she had a feeling Haley was just the woman to finally break her. The smart thing to do would be to cut her losses now. For both of their sakes.

And yet...

Cupid's arrow had struck Des the moment she first laid eyes on Haley. Ever since then, there was only ever one answer she could give.

"Haley Thomas, are you saying you want to be my Valentine?"

Haley's smile lit up her face. "I'd love nothing more."

11

HALEY

Des borrowed a UTV to drive Haley back to her cabin when it got late, and Val was sitting up waiting for her with the remainder of the bottle of champagne.

"Here you go, dearie, have a glass," she said, pushing an already filled champagne flute across the coffee table toward her. "And sit down."

"I take it you saw Des go after me," Haley said as she took off her coat and unlaced her boots.

Val playfully arched an eyebrow. "Indeed, I did. And judging by the time, I'm guessing you two patched things up."

Haley glanced at the wall clock above the kitchen sink. It was past eleven and she genuinely didn't know where the time had gone. Did she really spend three hours in that little basement room with Des? Well, time did have a tendency to get away from them.

She sat down beside Val and lifted the glass to her lips. "Mm, this is good champagne."

"This resort knows how to do hospitality," Val agreed, with a sly smile on the last word like Des was part of the package.

"Stop," Haley warned. "I already told you more about our first night than I wanted to."

"But there have been new developments," Val pointed out. "And I'm your bestie. You tell me everything."

Well, Haley hadn't had many love interests since she started working for *Traverse*. The only one she dated since she met Val had quickly come to be known as She Who Shall Not Be Named. That meant Haley had never had much to divulge on the subject of her sex life. Besides, they spent most of their time talking about Moska when romance came up.

Haley tried that tactic now. "Have you heard from Moska today? Did she decide whether to go to that party?"

Val just gave her a bemused look. "Nice try."

Okay, so it wasn't Haley's most skillful dodge.

"You don't have to give me details if you don't want," Val said, finishing off her champagne. "But last time you were with her, you came back with your heart broken. I just want to know if she intends to treat my best friend right going forward."

Haley set down her glass and threw her arms around Val. "Thank you for caring."

"Of course I care." Val hugged her back.

"We talked it out," Haley said, letting her go. "It was a misunderstanding – you of all people know the struggles of conveying tone in writing."

Val nodded, but she didn't look entirely won over.

"I like her," Haley said. She wasn't used to this much openness when it came to matters of the heart, and admitting that twice in one night was making her a little dizzy. Or maybe it was the champagne. "I'm pretty sure the feeling is mutual after all. We agreed to just enjoy the time we have together."

If she knew it was temporary from the outset, she could keep her emotional distance and it wouldn't hurt nearly as much if it didn't end in an unexpected, spectacular fireball like her last relationship. In fact, it was perfect – mutually agreed on terms that would allow them both to have a little fun without giving up too much of anything they weren't willing to lose. Right?

"Well, if she breaks your heart I'll break her face," Val said, getting up.

"Don't, it's so pretty."

Val rolled her eyes, but she was grinning. "I'm

happy for you. But this booze is making me sleepy so I'm gonna crash."

"Okay. Night, Val."

"Night, Hay." She put her champagne flute in the dishwasher and the empty bottle in the recycling bin. Then before she disappeared into her bedroom, she said, "Hayley?"

"Hmm?"

"Please don't ditch me for the whole week," she said. "I don't think I can handle being apart from Moska on Valentine's Day *and* flying solo to all these couples' events."

"I promise," Haley said. "Sorry for tonight."

"It's okay," Val answered. "You didn't miss much. I'm not sure Art would have wanted photos of a bunch of boomers learning to box step."

Over the next week, the resort came alive with romance. Every cabin in the row filled up, and the lodge was bustling every time Haley set foot in it. Everywhere she looked, couples clung to each other with permanent doe eyes.

She and Des had exchanged numbers before they parted ways the night of the dance lesson, and the next morning, Haley woke up to a message waiting on her phone.

Morning, beautiful. I'm working til six today but I'd love to take you to the ice skating rink after if you're free.

A smile came involuntarily to Haley's lips, and she actually giggled to herself as she responded.

I'd love to, but I'm more of a skier than a skater... you might have to hold me.

She didn't have to wait long for Des's answer.

Try and stop me.

Haley floated on a cloud all through the day, and got some of her best shots so far. There were so many more people at the resort now, all blissfully happy and deeply in love, it was impossible not to capture that energy on film. Impossible, also, to keep herself from getting swept up in Des's charming smile, the faint dimples that appeared every time she smiled, the way the world disappeared when she looked at Haley.

They went ice skating, and laughed until their sides hurt when they wiped out, landing in a heap on the ice. They got cozy in front of the firepit, and drank hot cocoa with little heart-shaped marshmallows that no longer made Haley scowl.

Haley and Val went to a wine and cheese tasting while Des was working, and then Haley and Des partnered up for a cooking class while Val simply observed and took notes. They made red velvet waffles with homemade chocolate sauce, strawberries and more of that incredible mascarpone topping that Haley couldn't get enough of. Haley just barely managed to restrain herself from scarfing it all down during class, and she and Des made good use of that chocolate sauce in private later.

Then, on the tenth, Haley, Val and Des went as a trio to a painting class.

"Sorry I've been monopolizing Haley's time in the evenings," Des said as they found three easels together. The room was set up in a semicircle, with the instructor's easel facing the class at the front of the space.

"It's no problem, as long as she's still getting good photos," Val said. "I get plenty of Haley time while you're working, plus I met a couple at breakfast the other day who are also from Chicago, so we've been hanging out a bit. They're engaged and planning a wedding in Barcelona."

"Fancy," Haley said. She knew Val was waiting somewhat impatiently for Moska to be ready for marriage, and that Moska thought their relationship just got done moving to 'the next level.'

"Yeah, but I'm not sure I'd want a destination wedding," Val said. "I'd want to be sure all my friends and family could be there."

"All right, everyone," the instructor said from his

easel. "Please make sure your water cups are full and you have an assortment of brushes at your station. We'll get started in a minute."

There was a second easel behind him with a completed painting on it – a pair of lovebirds sitting on a tree branch, the sky behind them splashed with the pinks and reds and purples of sunset. Des squirmed on her stool.

"Is that what we're making?"

"Probably," Haley said. "Don't you like it?"

"The painting is fine. What I don't like is embarrassing myself," Des said. "Pretty sure this is going to be a disaster because I do not have one creative bone in my body."

"That can't be true," Val said. "Everyone has the capacity for creativity."

"Says the writer," Des shot back.

"Hey, you didn't make fun of me when my skates flew out from under me the other day," Haley pointed out.

"Pretty sure you did that on purpose so I'd catch you," Des answered.

Haley laughed. "Tell that to my broken ass bone."

"Coccyx," Val interjected, ever the human thesaurus.

"Okay, everyone, let's get started," the instructor said. "My name's Trent and I'll be walking you through creating this painting tonight. Don't worry if you've never painted before – I promise it's easier than it looks, and if nothing else, you'll have fun." There were a few more nervous chuckles around the room from people like Des who doubted their artistic abilities. Then Trent said, "Everyone, pick up a mop brush and we're going to start laying down background color."

Beside Haley, Des picked up a paintbrush. "Don't laugh."

"No promises," Haley said, a grin already forming on her lips. She had more confidence in Des's abilities than Des appeared to, but there was just something about her – she instantly brought a smile to Haley's lips whenever she was around, and made Haley laugh with her whole body, in ways she hadn't done in years. Even if this wasn't built to last, it sure felt right.

12

DES

At the end of the night, Des wound up with a square canvas painted with two dark blobs that looked, from a great distance, like birds on a tree branch. At the last minute, she'd added a rudimentary heart above their heads because she didn't think the lovebirds theme came through without it. Trent had the nerve to come over and hold up her painting for the class to see, praising her choice to *think outside the box* with that addition.

"As in life, painting is not about following the rules," he said. "Sometimes you need to follow your gut or your heart instead. See where it leads you."

He put her painting back down on the easel, and Des resisted the urge to throw her coat over it. She'd been looking over Haley's shoulder the whole class and watching in amazement as she perfectly replicated each brushstroke Trent laid down on his own canvas. Her painting looked just like the example.

"You've got a hidden talent," Des said while they washed their brushes and cleaned up their areas.

"Only when there's someone walking me step-by-step through it," Haley said. "And look at your birds – they're cute."

Des chuckled. "They're blobs."

"Cute blobs," Haley insisted. "I bet you did better than you thought you would."

"Oh, stop trying to make me feel better," Des said, one hand snaking out to pinch Haley's side. She laughed and squirmed, and Des pointed back at Haley's perfect canvas. "I'm not artistically inclined, and I'm fine with that. You, on the other hand, are an *artiste*."

"It's true, I see some natural talent there," Trent said as he came near on his last loop around the room. "You should take an art class sometime if you enjoyed tonight."

Haley smiled, but she was looking at Des, not the instructor. "I did enjoy it."

Oblivious, Trent waved her up to his easel at the front of the room. "Here, I can give you a few online course recommendations to get you started." Haley reluctantly followed him, and he raised his voice to address the rest of the room. "That goes for all of you –

if you want to pursue painting further, I'm happy to guide you in the right direction."

Des turned back to the sink, watching the grays and browns of her blobs – err, birds – bleed off her paintbrushes and swirl down the drain. She was drying the brushes on a paper towel when Val appeared beside her.

"Did you have fun?" Des asked. She felt bad as she suddenly realized she'd barely spoken to Val all night, and hadn't even looked at her finished painting. She'd been so wrapped up in Haley, what little attention she had left went to trying to keep up with Trent's instructions.

"I did," Val answered. "You?"

"I'm clearly not the next Leonardo da Vinci, but it was an entertaining evening," Des said.

Val was already finished cleaning her brushes, and she just stood next to Des, her hands in the pocket of her hoodie. Des set her brushes aside and turned to her. Val had blue eyes like Haley, but hers weren't nearly so bright and luminous. In fact, it looked like there was a storm brewing in them.

"Everything okay?" Des asked.

Val glanced toward the front of the room, where Haley was still busy with Trent. Then she took her hands out of her pocket, crossing her arms in front of her. She lowered her voice as she said, "I just wanted to talk to you about Haley."

Ah, so this was the *protective bestie, don't hurt my friend* talk. Des had been on the giving end a time or two, but she'd never stayed with one woman long enough to be on the receiving end. At least not for a long, long time.

"You don't have to worry–" she started, but Val cut her off. She was a woman on a mission and Des could see it was best to just let her say what she needed to.

"Haley told me you two are, like, short-term dating, or something like that?" Val said with a frown. "Just while we're here on the mountain?"

"Yeah, basically." Des didn't quite know how to put it either. All she knew was that Haley had forgiven her for that quickly scrawled note, and she made Des feel something that she hadn't felt in a long time. It scared her, and honestly if Haley was a local, if there was the possibility of something long-term, it would probably be too much... but since their time was limited, Des was going to make the most of it. "It was her idea," she added.

"Well, I don't really like it, but Haley is her own woman and she can make her own decisions," Val said. "I just don't want to have to pick up the pieces when we get back home, so you better not make her fall in love with you."

Des opened her mouth, but there were no words. What could she say to that? *I'll try not to?* Because she had no intention of breaking Haley's heart, or her own... but who in the world had control over something like that?

"I know," Val went on. "You can't make that promise, and you don't know Haley like I do. Honestly, she's probably already in love with you because that's the kind of person she is. Once she makes up her mind about somebody, it's set. I see how she looks at you."

That made Des smile, but she could tell from the look on Val's face it wasn't meant to be a compliment.

"She doesn't open up easily," Val said, glancing toward the front of the room again. Haley appeared to be wrapping things up with Trent. "Her last girlfriend was a cheating piece of crap and she's still not over that betrayal. I've never seen her be like she is with you. You obviously make her happy so I'm not going to stand in your way. Just... please be gentle with her when it's time to go."

Those words were like a fist closing around Des's heart, and her chest was still tight when Haley came over and wrapped her arms around her.

"Ready to go?" she asked. "I've been thinking about that grapefruit Bellini you mentioned... maybe we can drink them by the fire at the lodge?"

"Sure," Des said.

"I'm going back to the cabin to make some notes about tonight," Val said. "Want me to take your painting with me?"

"Yeah, thanks," Haley said. "You could join us, though."

Val just shook her head. "You two have fun."

She gave Des one last, warning look before she gathered up two halfway decent paintings and her coat, then headed out. Des brought Haley her coat and put her own on, then picked up her blobs. The paint was so thick it was still wet in places, so she was forced to hold it out from her body as they walked, like a small child who couldn't wait to show Mommy what she made in school.

She'd have been embarrassed if she wasn't still thinking about what Val said. Des couldn't hold it against her – had the tables been turned, she would have issued the exact same warning. But no matter how she looked at it, Des knew the damage had been done. There was no way she could take back the time they'd already spent together, and she knew from the look in Haley's eyes every time their gaze met that she was just as enamored as Des was.

Basically, what Val was really asking was for Des to be the type of woman who was worthy of her friend's heart.

And Des didn't know if she was or not.

As Haley released her hand and jogged a couple steps ahead so she could open the lodge door for Des and her painting, looking back and smiling at her, she realized she wanted to try.

The next morning, Des woke up to the light streaming through her window rather than to the blare of her alarm clock. She had a rare day off – given how busy the resort was, she was pretty sure it had been a clerical error, but she wasn't about to point it out to Greg.

She kicked back her blankets and looked outside at the fresh blanket of snow that had fallen on the cars in the parking lot overnight. She lived in a small apartment building with ten small units, nothing special except for the proximity to the resort. Des didn't need much – a place to put her stuff and lay her head at night. Her parents lived on the other side of town, and a handful of people she'd gone to high school with had stayed in the area. Most of them moved on.

Des wasn't dead set on sticking around here forever. Once upon a time she might have been content to stay, but now, aside from her parents, there wasn't much tying her to Emerald Mountain. She just hadn't gotten around to figuring out where she wanted to go next. Then Joy had called and told her about the maintenance job at the resort, and she'd fallen back into complacency.

But she couldn't get *too* comfortable. After all, Greg could fire her ass any second, and some days it seemed like he really wanted to.

She took her time getting out of bed, put on a thick, fuzzy robe and shuffled her way to the kitchen. She had plans to meet up with Haley for lunch, but she and Val were busy this morning doing an interview with the resort owner so Des had nowhere to be til noon. She was just putting a pot of coffee on when she heard her phone buzzing on her nightstand.

She went back into the bedroom to grab it. *Joy Turner,* the screen said, and Des answered. "Hey, what's up?"

Joy was to Des as Val was to Haley. An acquaintance due to circumstance – two queer women growing up in a small town – and at some point she'd turned into a real friend. Now she was traveling the country with her gorgeous wife, Carmen. They'd met on the slopes here – there was something magical about the mountain, Des had to admit it.

"Not much, Carmen and I are in NYC right now," Joy said. "We're visiting her parents and sisters. The twins are in high school and I can't believe how much more grown up they are every time we see them.

Anyway, I just wanted to let you know I have vacation time coming up soon and we're planning some traveling. We'd love to come out to Emerald Mountain for a few days if you're free. Actually, I wasn't expecting you to pick up – figured you'd be working and I'd leave a voicemail."

"Greg hasn't fired me yet, if that's what you're implying. It's my day off."

Joy laughed. "You gonna hit the slopes?"

"Maybe."

"*Maybe?*" Joy's voice was so incredulous Des had to smile. She usually did take every opportunity to get out there on the mountainside. What was the point of living here otherwise?

"I've got plans in a couple hours," Des explained. Joy waited patiently – damn it, she was good at that – and Des added, "I've been hanging out with a resort guest this week."

She didn't need this to be a video chat to visualize Joy's eyebrows raising impossibly high. "You are? As in, seeing the same woman on multiple days?"

"Yes," Des said, trying to act casual about it, as if this wasn't the first time since...

"Adrienne would be proud of you," Joy said, and the name was like a needle jabbing into Des's belly. Surprisingly, it seemed to be a smaller gauge than usual – that was progress. Also, maybe betrayal?

Adrienne Gagnon was the most exotic, stunning and fascinating person who'd ever lived on Emerald Mountain – at least as far as Des was concerned when they met fifteen years ago. She'd moved here with her family when Des was thirteen – her father was a Silicon Valley bigshot who craved a more nature-based atmosphere like the French Alps he'd grown up near.

Des had been instantly smitten the moment Adrienne walked into her eighth-grade classroom. In fact, it was the exact same *take your breath away* moment as the first time she'd seen Haley. Adrienne had sat down in the desk beside hers, stars in those big, brown eyes, and they'd been inseparable ever since.

That is, until three years ago, when the lymphoma that had been taking over her body ever since Adrienne's senior year of college finally took her. All her father's money couldn't save her, and neither could all the love that Des had poured into her.

Cancer could go fuck itself.

"She never wanted you to spend the rest of your life mourning her," Joy said softly, and Des realized she hadn't responded. She'd gotten lost in her thoughts, and she was staring blankly at the windowpane instead of looking through it at the world beyond.

She forced her legs to move, going back to the coffee pot and pouring herself a cup, trying to be normal. "When's too soon, though?"

"Only you can decide that," Joy said. "But you've spent years denying yourself real human connections, aside from me, Carmen and your parents. I think that if Adrienne knew you found someone you care about, she'd be happy. In fact, I know it."

Des sighed. She'd been doing a pretty good job of locking Adrienne away in the deepest chambers of her heart for the last week because she *did* feel good when she was with Haley. Now that Joy had spoke her name, though, it all came flooding back to the surface.

It's just for four more days, she reminded herself. *It's not forever. You're not forgetting Adrienne.*

"Tell me about her," Joy prompted.

Des sat down at her small kitchen table and took a sip of her coffee. The guilt faded a little bit. She smiled when she thought about Haley. "She's a travel photographer."

"Exotic," Joy said. "You like that. And what, pray tell, does she look like?"

"Blonde, gorgeous blue eyes," Des said, "a bit like Evan Rachel Wood in *Westworld,* but without the period clothing."

"Hot, got it," Joy said, making Des chuckle. "Continue."

Des settled in, the memories of her beautiful wife slowly sinking back below the surface as she talked about the new woman in her life. There really was something special about Haley, but maybe it was simply the urgency of the situation. She was letting herself fall in love with this woman because she knew there was no chance of it lasting forever.

It was safe to have feelings for her. Feelings Des hadn't had in a long time. Feelings she realized, thanks to Haley, that she missed.

"She does have an over-protective best friend," Des told Joy. "I got The Talk yesterday."

"Mm, sounds familiar," Joy teased. "I like the bestie already…"

13
HALEY

*I*t was still dark out and already, Haley had been up for over an hour. Photography was all about capturing the light, so it wasn't often that she found herself up and on the job before the sun rose. Today, though, she didn't mind the lost sleep.

She was with a group of about two dozen hikers making their way up a snow-covered trail on the side of the mountain. The trees on either side of them were marked periodically with red blazes of paint so they knew they were still on the trail, and there was a trail guide at the head of the pack, making sure of the same thing.

Haley hiked alongside Des, who wasn't even winded and acted like tromping through six-inch snow drifts at the crack of dawn was something she did all the time.

"You're embarrassing me with your fitness," Haley teased her when they were about ten minutes into the hike and she was already huffing and puffing.

"Yeah, well, I'm guessing there aren't too many mountains back in Chicago for you to climb," Des answered. Then, with a wry smile, she offered to give Haley a piggyback ride.

"Showoff," Haley smirked back at her, although she didn't hate the idea of wrapping her arms and legs around Des and holding on tight. In any other context…

They were on their way to a lookout spot with a clear, easterly view. They were all going to watch the sun rise over the mountain, then hike back down to the lodge where breakfast would be waiting. A little way behind Haley and Des, Val was chatting with some of the other couples on the hike.

"I feel guilty," Haley admitted to Des as she glanced back at Val.

"About what?"

"I've pretty much ditched Val the last couple of weeks," she said. "Even though I promised not to."

It was already the twelfth – there were only three more days left of their trip, and the whole thing had sped by impossibly fast. If Haley had been asked to guess when she first arrived, she would have said that two weeks with a bunch of couples doing lovey-dovey things would feel like an eternity. And now, she was the one being lovey-dovey and leaving her travel companion out in the cold.

"She's been right by our side through most of the resort activities," Des pointed out. "We've tried to make sure she feels included."

"She's been missing her girlfriend, though," Haley said. "This is their first real Valentine's Day and they have to spend it apart, meanwhile I've been spending every spare second with you."

"Would you have rather spent the trip with Val, and never met me?" Des asked.

"Of course not!" Haley reached instinctively for her hand. They were both wearing thick winter gloves and she could hardly feel Des through the layers, but she held on anyway. "I wouldn't trade our time together, you know that. I guess the ideal thing would be if I could clone myself and spend equal time with Val... or better yet, Art could have just let Moska come on this trip with us like Val wanted."

"Yeah, but then if you *hadn't* met me, Val would be the one ignoring you and feeling guilty," Des said.

"True."

"I think Val is a good friend, and she's happy that you're happy," Des went on. She looked pensive for a moment, like she was thinking one thing and deciding to say another. "Anyway, didn't she tell you to live a little while you were here? We basically have her to thank."

Haley laughed. "She told me to keep an open mind."

Des wrapped an arm around Haley's waist, pulling her close until they were walking in step. She nuzzled her face into Haley's hair and whispered in her ear, "I like it better when you've got an open mouth, and you're screaming my name."

"Mmm, maybe after this?"

Des sighed. "Alas, I have to report for work. This evening, though?"

"Definitely."

The tour guide, who just so happened to be Greg's nephew, Ivan, brought everyone to a stop, calling loud enough that the hikers in the back could hear, "We're at the lookout. You can lay out your blankets wherever you want, but not too close to the edge." There were a couple chuckles at that. Ivan checked his watch and added, "The sun will rise in about ten minutes."

As the crowd ahead of them disbursed to various vantage points, Haley looked around. The lookout was a massive, flat boulder that created a wide break in the trees. It had probably been there for millennia, carved from the glaciers and worn smooth over the centuries.

"Wow, it's beautiful," she breathed, sensing more

than seeing the vast expanse of snow-covered trees in the valley beyond.

"Just wait til the sun comes up," Des said. "Where do you want to sit?"

They tracked down Val, who said she was fine sharing Ivan's blanket, then found a spot that was somewhat secluded from the rest of the group, tucked into a little alcove of pine trees. Des took their blanket out of the backpack she was wearing and snapped it in the air. Haley caught the corners and helped her lay it out, then they settled down on top of it, their backs against a natural curve in the rock, Des's arm around Haley's shoulders.

The sky was already starting to lighten, and Haley took in the view little by little as it revealed itself. The word *majesty* came to mind.

She glanced to her right, where the rest of the group was spread out, but she couldn't see them through the pines. "It feels like we're the only two people out here," she said, settling into Des's arms.

"Why do you think I picked this spot?" Des asked.

When the first shades of pink began to bleed over the horizon, Haley pulled her camera out of the backpack and crouched on her knees to capture a few dozen shots. She turned her lens on Des when she felt like she had enough nature shots, only to find her staring not at the sunrise, but at Haley, amazement in her eyes.

"What?" Haley asked.

Des smiled. "You're incredible. I love watching you work. Whether you're taking pictures or painting birds or trying not to step on my toes while we learn to waltz, you get this intense look of concentration on your face, like nothing else matters and the rest of the world has disappeared for you." She reached forward and took Haley's hand, pulling her closer until Haley set aside her camera and straddled Des's lap. "You've looked at me like that a couple of times and it makes me feel like the luckiest woman in the world."

"Impossible," Haley said. "Because *I've* felt like the luckiest woman for these past couple of weeks."

Des gave her a crooked grin. "I guess there can be two?"

"It defies logic, but there must be."

Des threaded her fingers through Haley's hair, her hands going inside the oversized hood on her coat as she drew Haley in for a kiss. Haley moved closer, until her hips met Des's flat stomach and their chests pressed urgently together. Even through the many warm layers of clothing they were both wearing, Haley could feel the firmness of Des's body, felt neediness building in her own.

And then she remembered there were two dozen strangers – and her best friend – just on the other side of a couple pine trees to her right. The whole world really had disappeared for a moment, and her cheeks reddened as she slid off Des's lap and snuggled into her side again.

"I can't believe I'm leaving in three days," she said.

Des squeezed her tighter. "Me either. I hate it."

They hadn't actually talked about Haley's imminent departure before. That wasn't part of the arrangement they'd agreed on, skipping past all the awkward *will they, won't they* stuff and simply being together the way they both desperately wanted. But it was impossible to skip the end. As much fun as it was to set aside every last one of her inhibitions and old wounds and just let herself fall for Des, this *would* end. And soon.

"I hate it too," Haley admitted.

"Can I ask you something?"

"Anything."

Des tucked a strand of Haley's hair back inside her hood. "How come there's no girlfriend waiting for you back in Chicago?" She cleared her throat and added, "That sounded rude, and I know your last girlfriend hurt you... but Haley, you're so wonderful. You're passionate and smart and funny and I love every second of being with you, not to mention you're fucking gorgeous and you make me come so hard I sometimes worry I might pass out."

Haley chuckled.

"So what are you doing out here, seducing a

woman you know you're going to leave in three days?" Des continued.

"I'm seducing you?" Haley asked. "I thought it was the other way around."

"I'm serious," Des pressed. She sat up so she could look at Haley directly.

Haley squirmed at the thought of answering, the desire in her belly turning into something a little less comfortable. "I could ask you the same thing, you know. Falling for a resort guest can't be a good life choice."

"Yeah, it's not," Des agreed. "I've spent the last couple of years intentionally choosing partners that were good for a one-night bit of fun. I haven't wanted more... until you came along."

"So I'm just special, then?"

"Of course you're special," Des said, kissing her again. Then she rose onto her knees.

"What?"

"I don't hear anybody else," she said. She got to her feet and stepped around the pine trees, then came back with a mischievous smile. "They're gone. I didn't hear Ivan say it was time to go."

"Me neither," Haley said, glancing toward the horizon. The sky was still splashed with pinks and oranges, like a living watercolor, but the sun was fully visible over the mountains. "Should we catch up to them?"

"We could," Des said, then dropped back down on the blanket. "Or we could stay here a little longer."

"Don't you have to start your shift soon?"

Des checked her watch. "Not for another hour, I've got time. I just want to be with you."

"Okay… but no funny stuff – it's way too cold to get naked," Haley said.

"Who said anything about getting naked?" Des asked. She pulled Haley to her, then tossed one of her gloves aside. Her hand was warm and welcome as it worked its way beneath Haley's layers and between her thighs.

14

DES

*A*n orgasm at the hands of a beautiful woman, with a gorgeous view on the side of a mountain was officially on Des's top five list of ways to start the day. Hell, she couldn't even think of any other contenders for the number one spot.

She and Haley lay in each other's arms, content and warm despite the winter air all around them, catching their breath. And maybe it was the oxytocin, or the view, or the fact that Haley's departure date was like a giant ticking clock hanging over Des's head, but she felt the urge to share something with Haley that very few people knew.

"You still want to know why I don't do serious relationships?" she asked.

Haley nodded against her shoulder.

"I haven't talked about this in years, except to my

best friend," she prefaced. "But I think you need to know, because when you leave, I don't want you to think that you were just some hook-up to me."

Her heart was hurting already. She spent so much time in the last three years trying not to even think about Adrienne, and for her to come up twice in two days... that was a cruel trick of the universe.

Or, as Joy would say, maybe it meant something. Maybe it was time...

She took a deep breath and held Haley a little tighter. "I was married once." She felt Haley's lungs expand as she inhaled. Des pressed on. "We met in middle school, and nobody expected us to last. Between her parents telling her that dating women was a phase, and mine telling me I couldn't possibly have found my soulmate in the eighth grade, they were all just waiting for it to fall apart."

"But it didn't," Haley guessed.

"Nope," Des said, a smile teasing at the corners of her mouth as the memories resurfaced. "We graduated and she went to Colorado State. College wasn't really my thing, so I worked for my dad for a few years, learned carpentry and construction. We got married the summer after Adrienne graduated."

"Adrienne... that's a beautiful name."

"Yeah," Des said wistfully. "Her family was French, and rich. I honestly think that was more of her parents' problem with our relationship – not that we were gay, but that I wasn't good enough for their daughter."

"I'm sure that wasn't true," Haley said.

Des smiled. She was thinking about Adrienne's mother scoffing at her inappropriate use of a teaspoon instead of a soup spoon at Thanksgiving dinner one year, and her father pulling Des aside to ask her when she was going to get a 'real job' – by which he meant one that required higher education. She didn't need to drudge all that up right now, though.

"We were happy in spite of them, for as long as we could be," Des said. She trailed off, knowing there was nothing left but the painful part of the story.

Haley linked her hand in Des's. They still had their gloves off, and Des's fingertips were starting to get chilly. Haley pulled her coat over both their hands to keep them warm. "What happened?" she asked softly.

"Adrienne was sick," Des said through gritted teeth. "Lymphoma."

"Oh god."

"Yeah. She and her dad put aside their differences and he threw every dollar he could at her medical care, which was fortunate because we didn't have great insurance," Des said. "Adrienne fought like hell and I never even saw her lose her optimism except for on a couple of really bad days. She was incredible, and so brave. I quit working for my dad to take care of her full-time toward the end, and I'm glad I got to spend that time with her. I was holding her when she passed."

"Oh god," Haley repeated, wrapping her arms around Des's waist. "I'm so sorry you went through that. I'm sorry that you lost her."

"Me too."

They sat in silence for a minute or two. Then Haley asked, "How long ago was that?"

"Three years," Des said. "Sometimes it feels like yesterday."

"I can't imagine a loss like that," Haley said, sitting up and looking Des in the eyes. "No wonder you're afraid to give your heart to someone again. Hell, I feel silly knowing I was going to tell you my sob story about my last girlfriend cheating on me and deciding to write off relationships because of it. How trivial."

"It's not trivial," Des said. "You deserve to feel how you do, no matter what anyone else is going through. I'm sorry you had your heart broken, too."

"Love stinks," Haley said, then cracked a smile. "Am I even allowed to say that here?"

Des couldn't help smiling along with her – that glimmer in Haley's eyes was contagious. "Probably not – I bet Greg has surveillance cameras in the trees. He'll have your entire cabin redecorated in the most obnoxiously heart-covered décor until you're back in the holiday spirit."

Haley laughed. "If there are cameras in the trees, saying 'love stinks' is the least of my worries considering what we did a few minutes ago."

Des hooked her arm around Haley's shoulder and kissed her forehead. "You're getting cold – we should head back. Are you hungry?"

Haley shook her head. "The buffet's probably ransacked by now anyway." She checked the time while they stood and Des folded up the blanket. "You need to get to work, anyway. It's fifteen til."

"Ah, shit," Des grumbled. "It'll take at least twenty minutes to hike back to the lodge. Gonna be in the doghouse once again."

"Sorry, I didn't mean to make you late." Haley helped her stuff the blanket into the backpack, then they started their return trip.

"Not your fault," Des said. "Anyway, I'm glad I told you about Adrienne. I've been thinking I probably should."

"How come?"

"So you'd get me."

Haley smiled. "I already got you. Pretty sure I figured you out while I was watching you deal with those people who almost killed us both sliding into the resort. You were so patient and kind, even when they deserved none of that."

Des chuckled. "Can I get you to write that on a comment card for Greg? I might need it."

They walked in silence for a few minutes. The sky was light and almost blue by now, the last pastel pinks fading away. Without the large group chattering all around them, it was suddenly peaceful in the snowy woods, and Haley and Des walked side by side.

Des was trying to imagine what was in Haley's head. How would she have reacted if the tables were turned and Haley had just told her the story of her tragically dead wife? She'd probably be a little scared, worried that she'd say the wrong thing and rip the wound wide open again. Maybe that was why they were walking in silence.

"I think I smell bacon," Des said, just to fill it, once the lodge was in sight.

"Yeah," Haley agreed. Then she took Des's gloved hand. "Wait up a minute."

"Hmm?"

"I know you're late so I don't want to keep you," she said, turning Des to face her. "I just wanted to thank you for sharing Adrienne with me."

Hearing her name in the mouth of a woman Des had spent the past week enthusiastically screwing and falling hard for was a unique kind of torture. She really could feel the fissures in her heart widening, like the cracks in old plaster on a cold day.

"I also wanted to say," Haley continued, "that even though I didn't know her, I'm sure she wouldn't have wanted you to be alone on this mountain forever. I don't want that for you either, and I just met you."

It was hard to breathe, and not just because of the cold air invading her lungs. "Stop."

"I'm just saying–"

"Please don't," Des begged. She wasn't ready for this, and thankfully, Haley seemed to pick up on it.

She nodded, and gave Des a hug she could hardly feel because of all the protective layers between them. "I care about you, Des. I want you to be happy."

Des nodded. She was in imminent danger of breaking into a thousand pieces, and the fight-or-flight part of her brain was yelling for her to get the hell out of there before her emotions burst forth.

"I care about you too," she said around the lump in her throat. "I need to get to the timeclock."

Haley nodded. "Will you text me when you get off work?"

"Of course," Des promised. Then they kissed, lips numb from the cold, and went their separate ways – Haley toward her cabin, and Des up the main road to the lodge. On the short walk there, she took deep breaths and practiced the thing she'd been doing successfully for the last three years – shoving thoughts of Adrienne deep down into the farthest chambers of her heart.

Putting her away for safekeeping.

Walling her off.

She was still in all her layers and starting to sweat when she reached the timeclock, about ten minutes late. She was reaching for the screen when Greg appeared in her peripheral vision, noting her tardiness.

"I thought we talked about this, Destiny," he said in his nagging tone.

And there it was – the final straw.

She whirled on him. "I don't know how many times I need to tell you, I go by Des, not Destiny. It's shorter, so it can't possibly be harder for you."

Greg's eyes widened and his mouth dropped open. Des knew she'd fucked up, but she was in it now – the ball was rolling.

"I am late, and I'm sorry for that," she went on, "but you know how many hours I put in here, and I do every single thing you ask. I don't think the mountains are going to crumble if I clock in ten minutes late, do you?"

Greg's mouth was still hanging open, and from the look he was giving her, it was entirely possible that no one had ever talked back to him like that before. He was used to an entire resort staff meekly following orders, no matter how ridiculous or nitpicky they were. On any other day, Des would have done the same, asking how high to jump and then grumbling once Greg's back was turned.

When he didn't answer her rhetorical question, she pulled a folded piece of paper from her coat pocket and waved it at him. "I have five more items on yesterday's to-do list, not because I was lazy or incompetent, but because no one can do this much work *and* answer to you every five seconds. So I'm going to go finish this list, and then I'll be back to get a new one, okay?"

The way she said it left no room for argument, and Greg just nodded. "Okay... Des."

She turned on her heel and marched back up the hall, her heart hammering in her throat, wondering if she was about to be fired. It wouldn't be uncalled for.

15
HALEY

That evening, Art insisted on a last-minute strategizing meeting with Haley and Val, going over the shots and notes they'd already taken and making sure their interview with the resort owner covered everything they'd need for the article. Not that they wouldn't have plenty of time to call the guy up and get additional information before next year's Valentine's Day issue. But they had only two more days left on Emerald Mountain, and if there was one thing Art hated more than the younger generation taking over, it was paying his staff to redo what he thought they should have done in the first place.

The consequence was that, thanks to time zone differences, Haley didn't get off her video call until after eleven o'clock at night, and she and Des decided to skip getting together that night and plan on dinner the following evening instead.

"She's gotta work early," Haley explained to Val. "Greg's running her ragged with all the Valentine's event setups on top of her usual work."

All that was true, and then there was the fact that they hadn't exactly left each other that morning on the best of terms. All day long, Haley had found herself thinking about everything Des had confided in her. Wanting to hold her and never let her go, if there was the barest possibility that she might find comfort in it.

And she'd been trying to offer sympathy when she said that thing about moving on. It seemed like after sharing all that, Des might be feeling guilty for how good the past week felt – like she was doing Adrienne a disservice by spending time with Haley.

But then she'd cut Haley off, becoming chilly and curt for the first time since they met. It almost felt like a physical slap, and Haley had walked away feeling awful for salting Des's wound, no matter how unintentionally. Who really knew what to say in situations like that? Losing a loved one, let alone a spouse, in that way was unimaginable, and Haley felt heartbroken simply listening to Des's story. Des was the one who'd actually lived it.

She just hoped the time of night, and Des's early

start tomorrow, were the real reasons why Des didn't make an effort to see her after her video call. She hoped she hadn't made things worse this morning by putting her foot in her mouth.

"You okay?" Val asked.

"Hmm?"

"You're frowning into your hot cocoa," she pointed out.

Haley's eyes focused and she realized Val was right. The mug she'd made before their call with Art had long since gone cold, and she was staring at the extra-rich dregs at the bottom.

"I don't think you can read hot cocoa swirls like you can tea leaves," Val pointed out.

"No, probably not."

"Something wrong?" Val asked as Haley hopped down from the kitchen stool where she'd been sitting and took the mug over to the sink. "Everything still going good with you and Des?"

"I think so."

"Uh-oh. I'm available to kick her ass if you want," Val offered, "although she's almost a foot taller than me so I'm not sure how that would go."

Haley chuckled. "I'm sure it's fine. We had kind of a heavy conversation this morning on the sunrise hike and we haven't had a chance to talk since then."

"Yeah, I noticed the two of you went off on your own," Val said. "I just assumed it was for... *other* reasons."

"Please, we're adults," Haley said with a roll of her eyes, even though that *had* ended up happening too.

Val didn't need to know everything about her, just as Haley really didn't need to hear the similarly themed conversations Val and Moska had on the phone before bed each night. For being a luxury cabin, the walls were surprisingly thin... thank God for headphones.

"You and Mosk on good terms again?" she asked. "Hopefully not going to miss her too terribly on V-day?"

"Ah, so we're changing the subject?"

Damn. Nothing got past Val. "Des told me some personal stuff, about her romantic past," she said. "I don't feel at liberty to share, but I'm worried I pushed her away."

Val nodded, studied her a moment, then asked, "Isn't that your MO?"

"What do you mean?" Haley's brow furrowed.

"Well, it's February twelfth," Val said. "Our plane leaves for Chicago in three days, and Des is staying here. I know you wanted to set reality aside and have a carefree couple of weeks with her, but you're not the type, Hay. You *are* the type to start looking for reasons to distance yourself, to wall off your heart so it hurts less when it's time to leave."

"Excuse me, I seem to recall you being the one encouraging me to 'keep an open mind,'" Haley said, hands on her hips. "Now you're telling me I never should have talked to Des because I can't handle a fling?"

Val just raised one eyebrow and crossed her arms in front of her chest. "That's not what I said – if that's what you *heard*, maybe you should think about that."

Haley let out a huff, then shook her head. "You're so much younger than me. I hate it when you're wiser, too."

Val came over and gave her a quick hug. "Just don't write her off before it's time. Don't make assumptions purely to keep yourself from getting hurt. Pain is part of life."

"There you go again, philosopher Val."

"Just call me Valistotle." And with that, she said goodnight then headed into her bedroom for her nightly call with Moska.

Haley donned her headphones, then crashed on the couch in front of the gas fireplace, her laptop propped on her knees. She'd uploaded the day's photos earlier, and she decided to go through the shots from the hike to see if the sunrise came out like she'd envisioned. Instead, she found herself staring for a long time at the snaps she'd taken of Des. Reclining on the blanket, her face lit up by the early morning sun, her eyes fixed on the camera – or the woman behind it – like that was the only thing in the world.

16
DES

*D*es spent most of the twelfth waiting for Greg to walkie her, asking her to meet him in his office so he could fire her for that little outburst at the time clock. When she finished her to-do list and reported back to the lodge for a new one, though, he didn't speak a word of it.

He just gave her a new list and said, "I appreciate your hard work, Des. We're in the final stretch for Valentine's Day, and then everything will calm down a bit."

And Des had wandered away slightly stunned. That was genuine gratitude without a single suggestion about how she should do her job, and furthermore, he'd used her preferred name for the first time since she started at the resort. She walked away from the encounter and immediately texted Joy to tell her about it, asking whether Joy thought Greg was having a stroke.

It's a Valentine's Day miracle, Joy had written back.

Des had to agree – there was no other explanation. So that was one regrettable outburst swept under the rug. All that talk of Adrienne had caused another, though, and every time Des thought about how she'd snapped at Haley, who was just trying to help, she cringed.

Those feelings had been compacted inside her for so long, they'd turned into a spring-loaded emotion bomb. When Joy brought Adrienne up, and then Des found herself being vulnerable on the side of the mountain with Haley, it had all come to the surface, susceptible to even the lightest touch. Des walked down off that mountain feeling raw and bare, shocked that she'd even been capable of telling Haley about Adrienne. Many a woman had tried and failed to open her up in the last few years, but with Haley, things were different from the very first glance.

That didn't mean it wasn't incredibly painful to rip herself open like that, and when Haley tried to tell her it was okay, it just proved to be one step too far. The pain boiled over and Des broke, and she hated how she spoke to Haley.

True to her nature, she ignored the problem all day.

When she got off work, she texted Haley and was mildly relieved to hear her say she couldn't meet up like they planned – she had to take a call, and maybe it was better that way. Des had bitten off more than she could chew, and she needed time to herself, to figure it all out.

They did agree on dinner the following night, when Des got done with her shift. Haley wanted to go into Emerald Hill to see where Des and most of the resort staff lived, to get an idea of what mountain life was really like.

I'll pick you up at your cabin about five, Des texted her.

I'll bring my camera, Haley answered.

So on the day before the big holiday, Des went to pick up her Valentine. She was still feeling a little raw and vulnerable, but she also couldn't wait to see Haley again. She retrieved her truck from the staff parking lot and slip-slid over a dusting of fresh powder to the row of luxury cabins.

She and Haley had just two more days together. Then this would be over, and she would be gone – nothing but a pleasant memory.

If she needed to repair the cracks in her heart, refortify her walls, she could do it once Haley was gone. Until then, Des wanted every minute she could with her.

Haley emerged from the cabin before Des had a chance to get to the door. She was wearing her big red parka, her camera hanging from her neck with the lens cap on, and she jogged down the cleared sidewalk.

"I'm so sorry about yesterday," she said as soon as they met at the end of the sidewalk. "It wasn't my place and I didn't mean to overstep."

Her eyes were so earnest, so deep with emotion, and her face bore the same lines of anguish that Des's had for the last twenty-four hours.

"You didn't overstep, I overreacted," Des said, pulling Haley into her arms. "I'm sorry too."

Holding Haley against her body, suddenly Des's chest was full and she could breathe again for the first time all day. She didn't realize it until she had Haley back, but she'd spent the whole day feeling hollowed out.

It was the same feeling she'd learned to live with after Adrienne died. Des hadn't even noticed that the ache had lessened for a little while.

Forty-eight hours left, she reminded herself. *Enjoy it while you have it.* She pasted on a smile. "I have the perfect evening planned for us."

"Oh yeah?" Haley let Des walk her to the truck and open the passenger door for her.

"I know you wanted the real Emerald Hill experience," Des said. "I figured we'd start with my favorite little café – it's a local favorite, and I've been going there since I was a kid."

"That sounds great," Haley said. "I'm starving."

"After dinner, as long as the weather holds, I'll take you on a walking tour of downtown," she went on. "There are shops that have cropped up to cater to the tourists, but there's plenty of small-town charm left too. Hopefully you'll still have enough light by then to take some pictures."

"And if the weather doesn't hold?"

Des winked. "Then we'll go back to my apartment and hunker down."

Haley smiled. "I like that option too."

"I thought you might."

The trip off the mountain took about twenty minutes – mostly because the roads were slushy from a few inches of mid-day snow. When they got to the restaurant, a cozy little place called the Powder Hill Café, the dinner rush was just beginning. Des had called ahead, and when the owner, Norma, spotted her, she led Des and Haley to a booth along the wall.

"And who is this?" Norma asked as they walked.

"This is Haley. Haley, Norma, proprietor, hostess, waitress, Jill-of-all trades," Des made the introductions. She didn't provide any further context about who Haley was, though she could tell that the older woman was dying for details. When was the last time Des came in here with anybody other than her parents? Ages.

"Nice to meet you, Des spoke very highly of your food so I'm excited to try it," Haley said, and Norma beamed.

"I'll put in a good word with the chef, make sure he does his best work," Norma said, then winked and added, "The chef is my husband, Bart."

Mercifully, she left them at their booth, and Des passed Haley a laminated menu. "She'll probably ask for your life story before we get to the dessert course. Everybody's a busy body in a small town," she apologized.

"I don't mind," Haley said. "It's flattering, actually. Clearly you don't bring all your hook-ups here."

"You are not a hook-up," Des said, scoffing at the word.

Haley looked at her menu for a moment, or pretended to. Then her eyes met Des's over the top of the laminated sheet, and she asked, "What am I, then?"

Des nudged her foot under the table. "You're my Valentine. Speaking of which... what time are you going to be free tomorrow? I made plans for us."

"Well, now I feel like a slacker because I was just going to go with the flow like we've been doing," Haley said. "What plans?"

"Why don't you just tell me when you're free and

I'll come pick you up?" Des suggested. "It'll be more fun if it's a surprise."

"Okay... well, Val and I promised Greg we'd be at the floral arrangement class at two," Haley said. "After that, I'm all yours."

"Just how I like you," Des said, capturing one of Haley's feet between hers under the table. Yes, despite the guilt and uncertainty, this felt right. If only she could hold onto Haley like this, and keep her.

What's stopping you? The question popped into Des's head with such suddenness it hardly felt like her own thought. It almost sounded like Adrienne's voice in her head, and she didn't know what to do with that.

It was a valid question, though. Haley had to go back to Chicago in a couple of days, but what was keeping Des on Emerald Mountain? A job she was only mediocre at, according to her boss, and her parents whom she already didn't see much of because of how busy she was with work.

Joy left this place for a woman, and she ended up happier than she ever was on the mountain. Des could do the same...

"You two have a chance to look at the menu yet?" Norma asked as she set a couple glasses of ice water on the table.

"Not yet, actually," Haley said, giving her an apologetic smile. "Give us another five minutes?"

"Sure thing," Norma answered. She had more than enough other tables to keep her busy, the little restaurant filling up fast.

Norma and Bart were the type of people who were lifers here. They were perfectly content in this small town tucked below a mountain. So was Greg, who made the resort his whole *raison d'être*. But Des?

She shoved the thought aside. Apart from all the memories of Adrienne she'd be leaving here, she just met Haley two weeks ago. If she followed her home to Chicago, a restraining order was more likely to follow than a happily ever after.

Des knew that the things she was feeling for Haley were real, and raw, and exquisite, but what about Haley? What if she was just having fun on vacation like they'd originally agreed on, and she was content to leave Des behind and go back to her life when this ended?

Des put the thought aside again and picked up her menu. No sense in thinking all these things now, not when the clock was ticking on their time together.

"The chicken parm here is incredible," she told Haley. "As is, well, pretty much everything."

17
HALEY

The food at the café really was delicious, and the weather was nice enough for Haley and Des to take their time wandering around the town afterward. It was quaint and charming, a little too small for Haley to imagine herself living there full-time.

"Do you ever get tired of small-town living?" Haley asked as they lost the light and meandered their way to Des's apartment.

"It has its inconveniences," Des told her, looping Haley's arm in her own. "Like Norma back at the restaurant wanting to know my business, and having to drive forty-five minutes to the nearest Walmart."

"The horror!"

"Fortunately, I think we're only a few years away from fully drone-powered delivery services," Des said.

"Then this town can have all the McDonalds and Whole Foods deliveries it wants."

"Mmm, forty-five-minute-old fries," Haley teased.

"Yeah, I know you're spoiled living in a big city," Des went on. "You get to try everything that's new before the rest of the country, and anything you could possibly want is at your fingertips."

"Everything except you," Haley said, and Des looked surprised.

"Are you gonna miss me?"

"Of course," Haley said. The words came out with such emotion that now Haley was surprised at herself. If Cupid's arrow had pierced her at the beginning of this trip, wasn't his magic supposed to wear off by the end of the holiday? It showed no signs of doing so any time soon. She rested her head on Des's shoulder as they walked. "What are we gonna do when I go home? Are we really going to forget about each other?"

"I don't want to," Des admitted, her voice soft and tentative. "We did agree this was just for fun, a temporary thing..."

"...but I have feelings for you," Haley finished.

"I do too." Des let out a sigh. "I guess... there's long-distance."

"It worked for Val and Moska," Haley said. "They're living together blissfully now... when they're not bickering like twenty-year-olds." She paused a moment, then added, "But they hated it the whole time they were apart."

"Yeah, I hear it's tough. But what other option do we have?"

Actually forgetting about each other and moving on with our lives, Haley thought. It was what they had planned to do, but now that the time was almost upon them, it seemed impossible. How could she forget Des? How could she ever have fooled herself into thinking she could?

They walked in silence for a few minutes and arrived at Des's building. She led Haley up to her apartment on the third floor, and after they shed their outer layers, Des pulled Haley into her arms on the couch.

"We could run away together," Des said. "Send in your resignation along with your photos from this trip, and become a freelance photographer. We'll travel the world together and see all kinds of exotic places. You'll take fantastic photos and sell them to *National Geographic,* and I'll find handywoman-type work wherever we go."

Haley smiled, vividly picturing the fantasy that Des was weaving. "We'll eat authentic local cuisine and explore whatever each place has to offer, and make love every night until we fall asleep exhausted in each other's arms."

"Sounds perfect to me." Des nuzzled against Haley's neck, kissing her. "And I can make that last part come true without leaving the couch."

Her hand snuck under Haley's sweater, sliding up her stomach and finding her breast. Des squeezed, and Haley let out a sigh. "If only."

"Why not?"

There were a thousand practical reasons, and Des knew them just as well as Haley did. But why bother tearing down the fantasy just to live in the real, boring, unfair world they'd already agreed to leave behind while Haley was in town?

"Okay," Haley smiled against Des's lips. "Let's do it. We'll run away together."

Des flipped the cup of Haley's bra down and the warmth of her hand against her bare breast instantly hardened her nipple and sent tingles between her thighs. Yes, this was right. This was all that mattered – at least for now.

Haley spent the night at Des's apartment, then Des dropped her off at the cabin in the morning with a kiss and a cheeky, "Have a good day, darling."

"Until tonight," Haley answered with a wink.

Inside, she found Val decked out head to toe in pinks and reds. Haley grinned. "Getting into the holiday spirit?"

Val shrugged. "If I can't be with Moska today, I'm at least going to have some fun with my wardrobe."

She was wearing a pastel-pink velour track suit with matching pink Ugg boots. She had little polymer heart earrings dangling just above her shoulders, and a matching headband paired with a tight ponytail. Haley couldn't help teasing her, saying, "I think I'll wear all black to counteract what you've got going on there."

Val just shook her head. "Don't even try to pretend your heart's made of stone, Miss Stayed-Out-All-Night-*Again*." She headed into the kitchen and retrieved two mugs from the cupboard. "I made coffee. Want some?"

"Please."

While they sat at the counter and sipped, Val asked, "What's Des got planned for tonight?"

"She won't tell me," Haley pouted.

"I'm sure it'll be romantic as hell," Val pouted right back. "At least she's in the same state as you."

"Is Moska going to that party?"

A smile played on Val's lips. "I talked to her this morning and she said she's not in the mood after all, so we're just going to video chat and have a long-distance Valentine's like we used to. I think she felt guilty."

"You got what you wanted, though."

"Yes, except now *I* feel guilty for talking her out of going to the party."

"There will be plenty more," Haley pointed out. "What's it like, long-distance dating?"

"Rough," Val said. "And a whole lot of work. I don't miss it, but it was worth it because now we're together and she's the one I want to spend the rest of my life with."

"Aww. Think you'll be able to convince her it's time for that step anytime soon?"

Val shrugged. "She's skittish, but her parents divorced and she just doesn't want to repeat their mistakes. She's worth waiting for." She turned to Haley, eyebrow raised. "Wait, why did you ask about the long-distance thing?"

She said it like she already knew, and Haley said, "Just wondering."

"Yeah, right."

"I gotta take a shower. We have about an hour before the flower arranging thing starts, right?"

"Yep."

Haley slid off the stool and headed down the hall

to get ready for the day. Valentine's, the big event that she and Val came here for. And instead of work, her mind was entirely on Des – what she had planned for tonight, how many hours stood between them, and what they were going to do when all this was over.

She didn't want it to end.

Time felt like it was crawling all day because Haley couldn't keep her mind off Des. When at last the festivities ended – or at least the ones *Traverse* was interested in – she brewed a fresh pot of coffee as a pick-me-up, then texted Des to let her know she was free.

I'm all yours was what she actually wrote, and her body was already vibrating with desire for her. Even though they'd ravished each other the night before, and once more in the morning before Des dropped Haley off, it seemed like no amount of fucking was enough to satisfy her. It was like an itch which, once scratched, only became more intense, more needy and insistent. It was an intensity she'd never felt before, and she loved it.

Craved it.

Craved Des.

By the time Des pulled up in front of the cabin in

her truck, Haley's heart was racing and her core was pulsing. *God, I hope she doesn't want to go out to eat,* she thought as she headed out the door, *because all I want to do is devour her.*

"Bye, Val, I'm out!" she called just before she pulled the door shut.

"Have fun!" Val shouted back from her bedroom.

Haley had felt a little guilty about leaving Val alone on the most romantic day of the year, but now that Moska was available, it was probably best that she make herself scarce. While Haley was getting ready for Des, Val left the cabin and came back with a fresh bottle of champagne, and she looked ready to have a romantic, if virtual, evening of her own.

"You too," Haley called, then shuffled as quickly as she could down the snow-dusted walk and hopped in Des's car. She knelt on the front seat, leaning in to give Des a long, lusty kiss, pulling back just enough to say, "Happy Valentine's Day."

"Happy Valentine's Day," Des repeated, kissing her again and running her hand down Haley's back, over her ass.

"I could climb across this seat and fuck you right here and now," Haley growled, nibbling on Des's lower lip. "Please tell me your plans don't involve going out in public."

"Hell no, I want you all to myself tonight," Des said. "Sit down, babe, we're not going far."

Haley obediently did as Des asked, and was rewarded when Des put her hand on Haley's thigh, then slowly inched upward to the crease of her legs. "I love this dress, by the way... I desperately wanted to do this the first time I saw you in it."

Haley was wearing the same velvet dress and tights she'd had on the night of the dance lesson, and she spread her thighs when Des's fingers pushed up her skirt and slid between her legs. They stroked up and down over Haley's swollen lips, through the fabric of her tights, and Des gave an appreciative groan.

"You're wet already."

"I've been thinking about you all day."

"Got yourself all worked up for me?" Des asked, finding her clit and applying pressure that made Haley squirm in her seat. "I can't wait to make you come undone."

"It won't take much," Haley admitted. In fact, she was pretty sure if Des kept rolling the pad of her finger over her clit just like that, she was going to come right there in the car. She bit her lip and Des seemed to sense how close she was getting. She backed off, preferring to let Haley suffer for the moment.

The ride was mercifully short. Des pulled the

truck to a stop again just two minutes later, in front of the last cabin in the row.

Haley looked at her, eyebrow raised. "Cabin twenty?"

"I rented it properly this time," Des said. "It's ours for the night."

They went inside, and Haley's breath caught in her throat. Not only did they have a warm, romantic luxury cabin all to themselves, Des had gone all out decorating it for the occasion. There were multiple vases of red roses on tables and counters around the common area, and Haley spotted a bottle of champagne chilling in an ice bucket near the already lit fireplace. And... "Are those mascarpone-stuffed strawberries I see?" she asked, eyeing a platter set out on the kitchen island.

"They are," Des confirmed. "I know how much you love them, so I got a buddy in the kitchen to make us a batch with the biggest, ripest berries she had. I thought maybe we could sip champagne and feed them to each other in the Jacuzzi tub."

"That sounds blissful," Haley said, looping her arms around Des's neck. They kissed, then she drew back to look into those big, brooding eyes. "You didn't have to do all this. I would have been happy just to snuggle up with you by the fire."

"I know, but I wanted you to have the full Emerald

Mountain Valentine's Day experience," Des said, then winked. "For the magazine, of course."

"I left my camera in my room," Haley admitted.

"I guess you'll just have to commit tonight to memory, then." Des unzipped Haley's coat, sliding it off her shoulders and tossing it toward the back of the couch. "Now, about that soak in the tub…"

18
DES

Des drew a bath, adding soap to make it bubbly, and Haley brought the champagne and strawberries from the kitchen. They popped the cork and took a couple sips, but the food was very quickly forgotten once they were naked and slippery together in the tub.

Haley was indeed very close to the edge, her whole body twitching with desire the moment Des laid her hands on her. She took great pleasure in pinning Haley to the wall of the large tub, positioning her over one of the jets and rubbing her clit with the heel of her hand as she plunged two fingers into her slick, hot core. Watching her squirm and moan, and her head fall back against the porcelain, was the sexiest damn thing Des had ever seen, and when Haley's breasts rose above the waterline, she took her nipples into her mouth.

Sucking the bathwater off them.

Teasing the pert flesh with her tongue.

Her own body giving little spasms of joy as Haley came undone beneath her.

You're mine, all mine, Des thought as Haley's sex convulsed around her fingers. *For tonight, for as long as I can keep you.*

Neither of them was willing to bring up Haley's inevitable departure, or ruin the fantasy that they would run away together after tonight. As far as Des was concerned, they were on the verge of starting their nomad life – Haley as an award-winning travel photographer and Des perfectly content to follow her wherever she wanted to go.

Which, for now, was the bedroom.

Once they'd exhausted themselves in the tub, they toweled off and Des handed Haley an incredibly soft, plush towel to wrap up in. She put on a second one, then grabbed the champagne and strawberries – maybe they'd get around to them once they were lounging in bed.

The bedroom, which they'd never made their way to on their first night in this cabin, was just as luxurious as the rest of it, and Haley grinned when she saw the extra touch Des had arranged – a trail of rose petals across the floor and scattered over the duvet.

"No one's ever bought me roses before," she

confessed. "Let alone made a trail of them into the bedroom."

"Well, all the other women in the world have lost their chance, because I want to be the only one buying you flowers now," Des said, scooping her into her arms.

"I only want flowers from you," Haley said, her words dreamy and warm just like her body.

Des bowed her head and kissed her, then trailed little pecks and nibbles down her neck. When she got to the impossibly soft curve at the base of Haley's neck, she nuzzled in there, breathing Haley in, memorizing her essence. Soaking up the feel of their bodies pressed together.

"I love you."

Haley stilled. "You do?"

The words had come out without conscious thought, escaping her lips just as easily as a breath, and she was surprised to find that no part of her wanted to take them back. "Yes. I really do."

Haley hugged her tighter, her lips brushing Des's ear as she answered, "I love you too. I think... you're my Destiny."

"I think so too," Des growled, "even though that is *such* an unoriginal line."

Haley squirmed beneath her. "I can't help it, you make my brain short-circuit."

Des balled into fists on Haley's hips, pulling at her

robe. Haley took the hint, loosening first her belt, then Des's. Their bodies came together, warm and soft and still slightly damp from the tub. Des wrapped her arms around Haley's waist, holding her like she never planned to let go. Then she dragged her over to the bed and tossed Haley down on it.

Haley let out a surprised laugh, but Des's eyes weren't on her face. She watched Haley's breasts bounce as she fell, and then her eyes trailed lower, to the light-colored, neatly trimmed hair concealing her sex. Des dropped to her knees in front of the bed and drew Haley's legs apart. Her pussy was glistening with need again already, swollen from the orgasms Des had already given her in the bath.

Every inch of her was beautiful, and delectable.

"I fucking love the way you taste," Des said as she dipped one finger between Haley's folds, separating her lips and making her moan.

"I love it when you taste me," Haley breathed, her body pulsing visibly with each heartbeat.

Des pressed two fingers into her, delighting in the way Haley squirmed with every thrust, then brought her mouth down to lap at her sweet nectar. She rolled her tongue over Haley's clit, alternating between broad, long laps and little circles with the tip of her tongue, knowing it would drive her to the edge.

"Oh my God," Haley gasped, her hips driving

down on Des's fingers, needily pushing her deeper. "Fuck me... please..."

She was goddamn insatiable tonight, and that suited Des just fine – she could stay on her knees until the sun came up, worshiping every inch of Haley's body and making love to her again and again.

She thrust deeper, harder. Haley bucked her hips and groaned, pressing more insistently against Des's mouth. It was all she could do to keep up with Haley's frenetic pace, lapping at her clit and adding a third finger to her tight little hole.

Haley came hard against Des's mouth, arousal flooding over her tongue as Haley's thighs closed on either side of Des's head. Her own body ached with the need to release as she reveled in Haley's cries, in the quivering of her thighs and the spasms of her pussy.

"God, you are the sexiest woman alive," Des groaned as Haley finally relaxed back on the bed. She kissed her way out the inside of Haley's thigh, then discreetly wiped herself dry on one of their discarded towels before lying next to her.

Haley was still breathing heavy, her legs flopped open as the last waves of her orgasm subsided like the ocean receding from the shore.

Des reached over to the bedside table for a remote and turned on a gas fireplace at the foot of the bed. She turned it up high enough to keep them comfortable lying naked above the sheets, and then she settled down beside Haley, hand going between her thighs and lazily stroking her until she was ready to come again.

"It's never been like this for me before," Haley said, planting little kisses on Des's lips, her chin, her jaw. "I've never been this... open... before."

"Oh yeah?" Des dipped a finger into Haley's core.

"Not like that," she said, then bit her lip and threw one leg over Des's hip. "Mmm, but that feels good."

"Like this?" Des asked, probing deeper.

Haley nodded, her hand going down between Des's legs and finding her clit. "Seriously, though... it's not easy for me to open up to people. I know my issues are unimportant compared to your past–"

"Nothing about your life or your feelings is unimportant," Des objected.

"You make me want to give my heart to you," Haley said. "I didn't just say I love you because I got caught up in the moment, or because you said it first... I do."

"I do too," Des said, repositioning her hand so she could thumb Haley's clit. Her own core was becoming molten with desire, closer to orgasm with each stroke of Haley's fingers.

"I'm not sure I've ever even been in love before – not for real," Haley said.

Des felt her pussy clench and knew she could

make Haley come in just a few more strokes. Her own body was kindling, ready to catch fire, and she set the pace, wanting nothing more than to come with this beautiful, sexy goddess.

She pushed Haley down onto her back, spreading her knees wide and then thrusting into her again with her fingers. "Don't stop touching me, I'm close," she said, her hips moving in time with the rhythm the two of them were creating. With her free hand, she reached over to the bedside table and pulled out the drawer.

"What are you doing?" Haley asked.

Des gave her a wry smile. "I brought toys." She reached in and withdrew a double-ended vibrator. "What do you think?"

"Yes, please," Haley breathed, her hips already bucking against Des's hand.

She clicked the toy on and brought it down between Haley's legs. She let out a gasp as soon as it touched her, and Des teased her clit with it for a moment – not too long because she didn't want to push her over the edge. Then she drew the toy through Haley's slick folds, lubricating it in her own juices before pushing it into her.

"Oh, fuck!" Haley gasped, her eyes fluttering shut and her hand stilling over Des's sex.

That was fine, Des loved to see Haley entirely consumed with pleasure, and she had something else in mind for them right now anyway. She took hold of the vibrator, drawing it in and out of Haley's core and using the other end to tease her own clit. They were both so worked up it only took a moment before Des's body was flooded with heat, an orgasm ripping through her while Haley moaned and thrashed as her own pleasure stole her breath beneath Des.

It had to be past midnight when they finally took a break, wrapping themselves up in robes and refueling with champagne and strawberries. Haley kept stealing glances at Des, coy ones she couldn't quiet read until finally she asked, "What?"

"I still can't believe you did all this for me," Haley said. "This has been the best Valentine's Day of my life, without comparison."

"I'm glad," Des said, kissing her forehead. "You deserve it."

Haley nuzzled up to her, nosing Des's neck before resting her head on her collarbone. "You do too." Des didn't say anything, so Haley looked up at her through her lashes. "I mean it... tell me to shut up if this is too sensitive a subject for tonight, but I got the impression the other day that you didn't think you were allowed to move on. I'm sure..." Haley paused over Adrienne's name, afraid to say it and open the wound anew. "*She* would want you to be happy."

Emotion caught in Des's throat and if she'd had any words, she wouldn't have been able to produce them.

Haley took her silence as permission to continue. In a matter of seconds, they'd somehow gone from suggestively nibbling on strawberries to Haley wrapping her arms so fiercely around Des's middle that she could hardly breathe. Haley was holding her and telling her all the things she'd been denying to herself all this time.

"Adrienne wouldn't want you to be alone," she said. "Not if she loved you the way you loved her."

"But..." Des's voice cracked and she fell silent, then tried again. "She was the love of my life, my other half... my soul mate. And I never thought I'd feel that way again – didn't think there was anyone out there who would make me want to. Until I met you... how can that be? What if I didn't..."

Again, her words failed her as her darkest, ugliest fears threatened to close her throat. Haley was still holding her tight, anchoring her, and it was as if she was inside Des's head because she answered like she knew what Des was trying to say.

"Loving me doesn't mean loving her less," she said. "I may not have much experience with genuine love, but I do know it when I see it, and when I feel it. Whoever said you can only have one soul mate, anyway?"

Des snorted. "Everyone."

"Well, they're wrong."

Des did her best to swallow all the emotion choking her, but the lump in her throat wasn't going anywhere. So instead, she turned Haley's face to her own and kissed her deeply. Kissed her like there was no tomorrow, like she could keep her forever.

The morning came far too quickly.

Des awoke to the alarm on her phone going off somewhere distant in the cabin, and Haley's perfect, naked body curled up against her. They'd made their way back into the bedroom after their midnight snack, and lay down in a tangle of limbs. They talked for a long time, fooled around whenever the urge struck, and at some point Des's eyelids had simply gotten too heavy to stay awake.

"Mmm, what time is it?" Haley asked, sitting up beside her.

Des kissed her lips, then the pert nipples peeking over the top of the sheets. "Must be about six-thirty.

You should go back to sleep – we have the cabin until eleven."

Haley shook her head. "If you're up, I'm up. You have to go to work?"

"Yeah," Des said, reluctantly slithering out from under the blankets. "You and Val are going back to Chicago today, right?"

There was no point in keeping up the illusion, maintaining the fantasy of running away together. It was February fifteenth and reality was calling to both of them. Still, a small voice in Des's head begged Haley, *Please say you'll stay, or bring me with you.*

But Haley was too practical for all that. She just nodded, and sat up. The sheets pooled around her hips, and she looked positively irresistible in the early morning light. "Our flight's at two," Haley said.

Des located her phone in the pocket of her pants and shut off the alarm, then crawled back onto the bed. "Do you have to be on it?"

Haley smiled, but there was an an apology in her gaze. "I can't stay here forever."

"Why not?" Des asked. Haley laughed, but Des pressed on, the urgency from last night rising again, hammering in her chest. "There are lots of freelance photographers in the world, and I can find work anywhere. We could do it."

"We could…"

"But?"

Shit. Haley was looking at her like Des was the one who'd gotten too attached after a one-night stand. It was uncomfortable and she hated knowing that she'd made Haley feel that way after their first night together.

"Art needs my photos," Haley said, "and Val's expecting me to go back with her, and... I'm scared."

"Of what?" Des asked, even though truth be told, she was scared too – fucking terrified, in fact.

"What if we break our promise to just keep this short-term and we find out this isn't real?" Haley asked. She lowered her voice and added, "What if it *is?*"

Des nodded. "I know. I'm scared of all that too. Come on, take a quick shower with me and we can think about what we're gonna do."

"Quick?" Haley asked, eyebrow arched.

Des grinned. "If I'm a couple minutes late to work, it's not like it'll be the first time, but at least it'll be for a good reason. In fact, maybe I should just quit right now and that way at least I'll have a few more hours with you."

"No," Haley shook her head. "Absolutely not. Whatever we do, nobody's torpedoing their life on a whim. That might work out in romantic comedies, but not in real life." She smacked Des's ass and with a wry smile said, "Now get in that shower, dirty girl."

They managed to actually get clean and have some fun before Des had to get dressed and hustle over to the lodge, and they decided that the only practical route forward would be to try the long-distance thing, at least for a little while. Haley would go back to Chicago and turn in her camera roll, and she promised to get advice from Val and Moska on making the distance feel smaller until she and Des figured out their next steps.

It wasn't a romantic solution, one with a big, sweeping grand gesture that ended with the two of them riding off into the sunset on a white horse. It wasn't something Des was excited about, exactly, but she had to admit it was the most logical thing to do.

So they left the cabin together a little after seven-thirty, the sunrise splashing the mountains with pastel pinks and oranges, and Des drove Haley back to her cabin. She got out of her truck so they could say a proper goodbye, holding each other extra tight just in case it was the last time.

"Come find me before you go, if you can," Des said. "But lord only knows where Greg will have me working today. Lotta clean-up to be done now that the holiday is over, you know?"

"I'll do my best," Haley promised.

"And if we don't see each other again today, call me when you land safe in Chicago," Des insisted.

Haley smiled. "I will. I can't wait to hear your voice again."

"Are you absolutely sure running away together is off the table?" Des tried one more time with a wry smile, already knowing the answer.

Haley laughed. "'Fraid so. I guess it's what you get for falling for a tourist."

"And you fell for a townie – rookie mistake," Des shook her head.

They kissed, and Des had to forcibly unlock her arms from Haley's waist. They kissed again, and again, and then when she had bare minutes to make it to the timeclock, Des finally – and reluctantly – let Haley go inside.

She got back in her truck.

Drove to the lodge.

Clocked in a couple minutes late.

And wondered if showing up for work today was the dumbest thing she'd ever done.

19

HALEY

She hadn't even packed her bags and already Haley's chest was aching, like she'd left her heart in cabin twenty.

Val was over the moon about going home. She was literally skipping around the kitchen, making coffee and heating up leftovers for breakfast, when Haley got back that morning.

"I get to see my baby again at last," she sing-sang while she retrieved mugs for herself and Haley. "And she told me last night she has a belated Valentine's surprise for me."

"That's sweet, Moska's a good partner," Haley said as she plopped down on a barstool. "Coffee please."

Val grinned. "Didn't get much sleep last night, huh?"

She filled Haley's cup, then her own, and leaned

with her elbows on the island in the universal gesture for *dish, please.* Haley just smiled at her.

"You're not a kiss and tell kind of girl, are you?" Val asked, the disappointment obvious on her face. "Just tell me – was it as romantic and sexy as you hoped it would be?"

Haley's grin turned coy. "Let's just say if I were writing the review for this place, I'd give it five stars as a Valentine's destination."

"Maybe you *should* write the review," Val said. "You're the one who fell in love here, after all. I just had a bunch of sad phone sex with my girlfriend."

Haley laughed. "If it's any consolation, I think sad phone sex might be in my future."

Val's eyes got wide and her smile spread across her face. "Does that mean you're actually in love?"

"I think I am," Haley said, not because there was any real doubt left in her mind – more because it all still felt so surreal. "We're going to try the long-distance thing for a while."

She was pretty sure from the way Des had talked the last few days that she could have asked her to hop on a plane and come back to Chicago with her today. She secretly loved knowing there was someone who wanted her enough to follow her across the country. But the last thing she wanted was for Des to move for her and then resent her if they didn't work out.

Haley still wasn't convinced she was worth moving for.

So they'd take things slow, and make sure they were really ready for the next step... whatever that might be.

Val had no such motivation to be cautious. She flew around the kitchen island and threw her arms around Haley, bouncing up and down as they hugged. "I'm so happy for you! She's gonna come visit, right? We're definitely double-dating."

She managed to pull some details out of Haley about their Valentine's date – reluctantly at first and then with gushing admiration for how much work Des had put into the whole thing. When Val had settled down a bit and gone back to her breakfast, a day-old English muffin she'd snagged from the continental breakfast bar, Haley asked what she thought Moska's surprise was.

"I hope it comes in a box about this big," Val said, miming a ring box.

"You really think she'd propose?" Haley asked.

Val shook her head. "Pretty sure I'm the one who's going to pop the question when the time comes... but a girl can dream. I've been ready basically since the day she set foot in Chicago." Haley raised her eyebrows in surprise and Val added, "When you know, you know."

That, she could agree with.

Never in a million years would she have predicted that this trip would result in anything but some pretty photos for the magazine – maybe a cover image, if she was really dreaming big. But when Des told her that she loved her, Haley knew in her heart that she loved her back, with everything she had.

Haley looked for her when she and Val emerged from the cabin. She texted her, *where are you?* But Des must have been busy. Haley could just picture her up on the archway, taking down the string lights that had first brought them together. She was just accepting the fact that she would leave Emerald Mountain without seeing Des again when she and Val went to the lodge to check out and Haley spotted her paramour in the lounge.

One more chance to kiss her, hear her voice, breathe her in!

"There's Des," Haley told Val breathlessly. "I'm going to say bye."

"Okay, but the airport shuttle is leaving soon," Val said. "We can't miss it."

"I'll be quick," Haley promised. She left Val at the front desk, where the overenthusiastic resort manager was taking one last opportunity to suck up.

Des hadn't seen Haley enter. Her back turned to Haley as she headed into the lounge, and Haley had visions of running up behind her and putting her hands over Des's eyes. It was the kind of middle school stuff that she never did while all her straight friends were effortlessly exploring their first loves. They had no idea how easy they had it in their boring, heteronormative little suburb.

Doing it now would be cheesy, but Haley was pretty sure Des would love it.

Des turned a corner and a cute blonde immediately threw her arms around her neck. Haley froze in her tracks.

No, couldn't be. Des was greeting a friend, or maybe one of her past flings was a guest and Des was about to gently push her off, tell her she was off the market. She'd set that woman straight soon enough.

Then Des wrapped her arms around the woman's waist and lifted her into the air, twirling her in a circle. Another cliché move Haley would have loved if it were her... but who the hell was this?

Des set the woman down, her back still to Haley. She watched the blonde kiss Des's cheek and decided she didn't want to see any more. She turned around and beat a hasty retreat.

What... the... fuck?! Haley could barely see through a film of tears as she returned to the lobby. She refused to let those tears fall, swallowing them as best she could as she stormed past Val and into the cold.

"I'm waiting outside," she said as she went, hoping her words were intelligible.

"Hay? What's wrong?" Val called after her.

How could she be so stupid? She bought into every sweet nothing Des fed her for the last two weeks, letting herself fall in love for real even when she knew damn well it was an awful idea. She'd believed Des when she said she loved her, and damn her fragile, dumb little heart, Haley loved her too.

Like she'd never loved anyone before.

Haley sat down on a half-frozen bench outside the lodge, and Val appeared a minute later, lugging the bags they'd left at the check-out counter.

"Haley?"

"The shuttle's coming soon, right?" The sooner the better. Haley was about ninety-five percent sure Des hadn't spotted her, but the last thing she wanted was some ugly scene on her way out. Or worse, for Des and her new flavor of the week to come outside and find Haley on the verge of tears.

"Any minute," Val confirmed, sitting down next to her. She yelped and stood back up. "That bench is ice-cold!"

"I hadn't noticed."

"Hay, what is going on?" Val asked. "Did something happen with Des?" Haley was doing everything in her power not to meet Val's gaze, but she managed to use her best friend power to read her mind anyway. "Seriously, what did she do?"

"Nothing," Haley bit out, relief washing over her as she spotted the shuttle van rounding the corner. "It's my fault – I let myself think what we had was real, even though I knew better from the start. Now I just want to get out of here."

The van pulled to a stop in front of the bench and Haley was the first in line to get on. She refused to say any more about what happened, even though Val asked several more times on the way to the airport. Sometime around boarding, she finally gave up and simply offered Haley her shoulder to cry on.

"When you're ready, I'm here to listen," she said.

"You're a good friend," Haley told her, and she didn't say a word for the rest of the flight.

20
DES

*I*f Des were the type of person to keep a diary where she scrawled all the most important things that happened to her, today would certainly have been a long entry.

She was still reeling from her night with Haley, trying to catch her breath from all the mind-blowing sex at the same time as her heart struggled to process the emotional side of things. They loved each other! But Haley was going home. But they would make long-distance work! But Des still had some lingering guilt about Adrienne to work through...

And then she'd been trying to be a good employee and put all that out of her head for the duration of her shift when she ran smack into Joy Turner – the prodigal friend returned!

"What are you doing here?" Des asked as Joy threw her arms around her. "I thought you were coming next week."

"We were going to go down to Florida to see my folks and then come up here, but Carmen found us a really good deal on plane tickets," Joy said, "so we're doing the trip in reverse. Damn, I've missed your face, friend!" She planted a cheesy kiss on Des's cheek then pinched it for good measure.

"Where is that wife of yours?" Des asked, looking around.

"Bathroom," Joy said. "We came straight from the airport and I think she's had to pee since we flew over Ohio."

"Going to get some skiing in while you're here?" Des asked. That was how Joy and Carmen had met – literally colliding on Emerald Mountain at Christmastime a few years ago.

"I think in my condition, that would be ill-advised," Carmen's voice came over Des's shoulder.

She turned around and her eyes widened as she took in the small but definite curve of Carmen's belly. "You're not."

"I am," Carmen beamed. "We're due in August!"

Des turned to Joy and slugged her on the arm. "You didn't tell me?!"

Joy laughed, glowing just like her pregnant wife as she took Carmen in her arms. "Our fertility doctor said it was a good idea to keep things quiet until the second trimester, just in case."

"Only our immediate families know, I swear," Carmen said. "We only told my sisters last week."

"Okay, in that case, I'm honored," Des said, drawing them both into another round of hugs. "And I'm really happy for you."

"Sounds like you've got your own things to be happy about lately," Joy said.

"Can we meet her?" Carmen interjected. "Did we make it?"

Joy laughed. "Okay, so there was a second reason why we changed our travel plans. I told Carmen about Haley and, well, here we are."

Des frowned and checked the time on her phone. She had a missed text from Haley, trying to find her, but that was from an hour ago. The airport shuttle, which ran on a very punctual two-hour loop, would have left just a couple minutes ago. Des had actually been in the lodge specifically because she was hoping to bump into Haley one last time before she left, and then she'd been sidetracked by Joy.

"I think you just missed her," she said. "But let's check to be sure."

"Damn, I thought you said she had an afternoon flight," Carmen said as she and Joy followed Des to the registration desk.

"She does, but you know how long it takes to get through airport security," Des said.

They had, indeed, missed Haley by a matter of minutes, and Des's heart sank – partly because she loved the idea of introducing her new girlfriend to her old friend, and partly because she'd been harboring a secret hope that Haley wouldn't get on that shuttle van at all. But she had – she was responsible and she had obligations in Chicago, and Des understood.

"To be completely honest, I'm not Greg's favorite employee," Des said, her voice low just in case he was lurking nearby. "I would not be completely shocked if he fires me when my probation ends. Would it be crazy to follow Haley to Chicago if he does?"

Joy just grinned. "Oh man, you've got it bad."

"You should just pull a rom-com and chase her to the airport," Carmen said. "You clearly want to."

"I do... but I'm also in this for the long haul," Des said. "I can't very well let her think that I'm the clingy, obsessive type and turn her off completely."

Joy was still smiling at her, and she clapped Des on the shoulder. "I haven't seen you like this since Adrienne. That look in your eye – that sparkle I haven't seen in so long? That's how I know it's real."

"It's... strange. And wonderful," Des mused. Then she punched Joy's arm again, lighter this time. "Anyway, stop making me mushy. I get off work at six. Dinner?"

"Absolutely," Joy promised.

"Can't wait," Carmen added, and then the two of them headed arm-in-arm over to the fireplace to warm up.

Des stood there admiring them for a moment longer, her heart full for the little family they were starting, the future they were building. She could actually see something like that for herself, with Haley in the picture. For the longest time after Adrienne died, there had been no future for her – it was just black. And now, she saw light. Warmth. Hope.

With a quick look around to make sure Greg wasn't nearby, Des pulled out her phone and sent Haley a quick text. *I miss you already. Safe travels!*

She tucked her phone into her pocket and did her best to have a productive day of work.

Des met Joy and Carmen at the Powder Hill Café after her shift. She was going to suggest they eat at the resort restaurant since the chef had been doing some amazing things with the menu since last Joy had been there, but no Emerald Hill native could resist the allure of Bart's homestyle cooking.

As soon as they walked in the door, Norma fawned over Joy and the fact that Carmen was now eating for two. That took quite some time, and involved a couple other locals who came over to their table to say hi. While Des waited for things to simmer down, she checked her phone.

She'd sent Haley just one more text, when she calculated she was due to touch down in Chicago. Des didn't want to inundate her with messages and overwhelm her, but she was surprised by how much she could already feel her absence. It physically hurt, knowing she was in a whole other time zone, and Des was craving the sound of her voice, or even the ping of a new message, if she couldn't have anything else.

No new messages, though. Des frowned.

"What's wrong?" Carmen asked, glancing over her shoulder.

"Nothing," Des said, putting away her phone. "I haven't heard from Haley yet, but she's probably still on Airplane Mode."

After approximately one eternity, with Des yawning and Carmen's stomach audibly rumbling, Norma took their dinner order and left them to talk in semi-privacy.

"Good old Powder Hill," Joy said. "Five bucks says Norma's going to give Bart every last bit of gossip *before* telling him our dinner orders."

"That's a losing bet, no thanks," Des said.

"Okay, enough chit-chat," Carmen interrupted, leaning forward on the table. "Tell us everything there is to know about Haley, how you two got together, and what it's like to join the 'I fell in love on Emerald Mountain' club."

Des smirked at her, but she couldn't help smiling at the opportunity to gush about Haley. It wasn't in her nature – except when Carmen and Joy drew it out of her. By the time their drinks and a warm basket of fresh bread arrived on the table, she'd recounted the last two weeks in a breathless stream of events, embraces and emotions she'd been so sure she would never feel again.

By the time their meals arrived, Des was feeling slightly dizzy from all the sharing, and all the attention. "We've got plenty of time while you're in town to talk about me and Haley – right now, I want to know more about this *massive, life-altering decision* that you've been keeping secret," she said, nodding toward Carmen's belly. "I totally understand why you kept it to yourselves, but now that I know... tell me more! How exactly does one decide they are ready to become a parent?"

The very idea sent tingles down Des's spine, and she couldn't decide if they were tingles of fear or anticipation.

Joy just shrugged. "When you know, you know."

Des rolled her eyes. "Why does everyone say that?"

"Because it's the truth," Carmen laughed. "And also, Joy's an assistant manager now, so we've been doing less traveling, living less like nomads. I think we started to settle down subconsciously because we knew it would be necessary for when we start our family."

"Will you miss it?" Des asked.

"There's always vacation," Joy said, putting a hand gingerly on her wife's stomach. "And I can't wait to see the world through our kids' eyes too – it'll be like starting all over again."

"Joy just wants to teach them how to be little badasses on the slopes," Carmen said.

Joy grinned in agreement. "You ever see a toddler on a snowboard? It's adorable *and* impressive."

"I've seen lots of toddlers on snowboards," Des reminded her. "In fact, I was one."

"And I'm sure you were adorable," Carmen said.

"You two are going to be awesome parents," Des said. "If Greg doesn't fire me, I'll make sure you get season passes with an employee discount for the little future ski pro."

"Greg won't fire you," Joy said, waving her hand.

"He's in everybody's business all the time but he cares about people. Look at how he treats Ivan – that kid is an idiot and Greg keeps him around, nephew or not."

"Ivan's grown up a lot this year," Des said. "He's really stepped up this past season."

They talked until the café's dinner rush ended, and passed around their plates to share. Joy and Carmen got their fill of Emerald Hill's finest, and then Carmen yawned. "Growing a human inside of you is tiring work. I'm not being too much of a party pooper if I want to head back to our room now, am I?"

"Of course not," Des said.

"Come on, I'll draw you a bubble bath," Joy said, getting up and holding out her hand to help her wife from the booth. Carmen swatted it away.

"I'm three months pregnant, not nine," she said. "Save that for when I feel like I'm smuggling a watermelon."

"Tread carefully with your response," Des teased Joy.

They parted ways with another round of hugs and plans to get together the following day when Des was done with her shift. At least having Joy and Carmen around would distract her from how much it sucked not to have Haley within reach anymore.

Des drove the short distance back to her apartment and shed her winter layers, then crashed on the couch.

She even undid the button on her pants, vowing never to try to keep up with a pregnant woman again. There had been way too much food on that table. Then she picked up her phone and checked her messages.

Still nothing from Haley.

Des hit *Call* and put the phone on speaker, relaxing while she waited. It rang and rang, then went to voicemail. Des frowned.

Haley had certainly landed in Chicago by now. Even if there had been weather delays or other airport fuckery, she'd be home now. And Des reached her voicemail, so the call had gone through – Haley wasn't in Airplane Mode.

For a few heart-thumping moments, Des's mind went to a dark place. One filled with fiery crashes, emergency crews, and no survivors. Plane crashes were exceedingly rare, but so were the odds of losing the love of your life to cancer in your twenties. Sometimes Des wondered if the universe just hated her guts, and by extension, anyone she loved.

She did a quick Google search, then scanned Twitter just to be sure. There was absolutely nothing in the news about a plane crash, or even weather delays.

"Stop catastrophizing," she ordered herself, then set her phone down on the arm of the sofa.

Chances were good that Haley had simply fallen

into bed after her flight. Des had certainly done everything she could to tire her out over the past two weeks. She'd hear from Haley in the morning, when she was rested, chipper, and hopefully missing her terribly. Des closed her eyes and promptly fell asleep.

21

HALEY

On Monday morning, Haley was back at her desk in the *Traverse* offices. She'd slept most of the weekend and yet she still felt jet lagged – or, more accurately, hung over from her star-crossed romance. Every corner of her heart still ached for Des, still loved her just as much as she had the day they left Emerald Mountain.

But she couldn't get the image of Des with that other woman out of her mind. She didn't even have the decency to make sure Haley had left before she moved on to her next fling. Or, hell, for all Haley knew, that was her girlfriend returning and everything Des told her had been a lie. Maybe Haley was the other woman, the homewrecker.

That possibility turned her stomach.

The only truly surprising thing was the fact that

Des kept trying to contact her. She'd stepped off the plane to a 'miss you' text, and she'd gotten a few voicemails and a couple more texts since then. Haley didn't have the heart to listen to the voicemails, but she'd grudgingly read the texts.

You get in okay?

Are you home safe? You're making me nervous, babe.

Everything all right?

What was she even doing, trying to keep Haley on the hook in case she had the opportunity to seduce her again in the future? Wasn't it enough to make Haley fall for her in the first place, crafting the perfect circumstances to make her lose herself entirely, just to, what, stroke her ego? Have a little fun? And now she wanted to string Haley along.

"Fuck that," she grumbled as she silenced her phone and laid it face-down on her desk. She opened her email and got caught up on what she'd missed, then spent most of the morning going through the digital prints from the resort.

There were a hell of a lot of Des pictures in the mix. Too many.

Haley tried to skip past them as fast as she could, or drag them into the trash. She wouldn't choose to look at the photos from the trip at all if Art hadn't been breathing down her neck from the moment she got off the plane, eager to pick out the best shots for the article. As if it was running next month instead of next year.

"Hey."

Haley looked up, blinking to clear the glaze from her eyes as she realized Val was standing at her desk. "Hi."

"Brought you a coffee," Val said, setting it down. Then she pulled an empty office chair over and sat down beside Haley. "You look like hell."

"Thanks," Haley said, taking a long sip. "For the coffee, I mean."

"Are you still not going to tell me what's going on?" she pouted. Haley hadn't said much on the train ride from the airport, and she hadn't felt like responding to anyone else's messages this weekend either. All she was able to handle was a brief call to her parents to assure them she'd gotten home safely – and a bit of guilt for not extending Des the same courtesy.

Which was, of course, quickly surpassed by anger at the fact that Des was capable of making her feel guilty. She didn't deserve it – and for all Haley knew, asking if she was okay was simply a ploy to get her talking. She'd been with cheaters and manipulators before and she knew all their games. It was just too bad she hadn't seen Des's true nature until it was too late.

"I'm sure I can guess," Val went on, snatching

Haley's phone before she could stop her. She turned it over, and her eyes scanned down the notifications on the screen. "Okay, so she's not apologizing... is that why you're not answering her?"

"She doesn't know I saw," Haley finally admitted.

"Saw what?" Val asked, exasperated.

Haley took another sip of her coffee. This time it tasted bitter and she set the cup down with a huff. "I saw her kissing another woman in the lodge when I went to say goodbye. She moved on just like that, like I was nothing." Now that the words were out, they just kept coming. "And I let myself be duped! I'm way more pissed at myself than I am at her. She told me from the start she didn't do serious – I'm the one who went and fell in love."

"Just because your last girlfriend was a cheating piece of crap doesn't mean you have to spend the rest of your life putting up walls and expecting people to treat you like that," Val said.

"I was stupid."

"You were happy," Val countered. "That counts for something."

"Yeah, a bunch of painful memories," Haley said, fully aware that she was wallowing and unable to stop herself. The wound was too fresh. Maybe it was a little bit of reopened old wounds too.

"So, if she was so eager to move on, why's she still texting?" Val asked.

"I have no idea," Haley admitted. "Probably because she doesn't realize she's been found out."

"Do you want me to text her?" she offered. "Tell her to fuck off forever? Because she hurt my best friend and it would give me great pleasure to do so."

Haley briefly considered it.

"Not," she said. "I think I should tell her that myself."

"Well, if you need moral support, just let me know," Val said, standing up. "I better get back to writing before Art gets on my case."

"I'm narrowing down my favorite shots to go with," Haley said, eyeing the full trash icon on her desktop. "I'll send some options over in an hour and you can decide which ones match the article best."

"Okay." Val set Haley's phone back on her desk, forgetting to flip it screen-down. "She doesn't deserve you."

"Thanks," Haley said. "For the coffee, I mean."

She stole a glance at her lock screen, and the handful of unread messages waiting for her. For the moment, she felt more anger running through her veins than despondency, and before she lost the nerve Val had given her, she picked up the phone.

Stop contacting me. It's obvious that Cupid's arrow has struck someone else – thank you for a lovely week–

Haley's lip curled as she typed that last part, thinking of the note that Des had left her after their first night in cabin twenty, the way it felt like she'd brushed her off the next morning. Des had sweet-talked her way out of that, and what she said made sense. But hadn't Haley's ex also had a whole bunch of excuses ready when Haley caught her cheating?

Was that note a red flag Haley dismissed? Had Des been showing her true nature from the start, and Haley ignored it because she was so busy falling in love?

She deleted *thank you for a lovely week*. With her luck, Des would miss the heavy sarcasm and think Haley was genuinely thanking her. Instead, she just hit Send. Then, with what little willpower she had left, she blocked Des's number.

"Okay, that's done," she said aloud, with much more confidence than she actually felt.

She turned back to her computer and tried to work, but she couldn't focus on anything except the ache of knowing she'd never hear from Des Grove again.

22

DES

Des's relief at seeing a text from Haley was swiftly discarded as she read the message and her jaw dropped.

Cupid's arrow struck someone else? What the hell did that mean? The first time she read it, Des thought Haley was telling her she'd found someone else. What, on the three-hour plane ride? No, that couldn't be it.

So she thought Des was the one who'd moved on...

"Oh shit," Des said, the pieces of the puzzle coming together.

The only women she'd even spoken to in the last twenty-four hours were Joy and Carmen, and Joy always had been the heart-on-her-sleeve type. Haley must have seen Des hugging one or both of them in the lodge. Of course she would jump to the conclusion that the interaction had been romantic – Des herself had told Haley that she'd spent the last three years coping with her wife's death by sleeping around.

"Shit," she muttered again.

She was currently in the middle of her shift, taking a quick coffee break to warm up after driving all over the resort taking down Valentine's decorations. But it didn't matter that she was on the clock – correcting this easily explainable misunderstanding was far more important than taking pink string lights to the basement.

Des hit Call, hoping Haley would answer the phone this time.

It rang once, then she got an automated message. "The number you have dialed is unavailable at this time."

Des's heart sank into her stomach. Did Haley block her? She ended the call and tried to send a text. *Hey, did you see me hugging someone before you left? That was Joy, the friend I told you about – she came to visit.*

Please, please read it, Des prayed, watching as the message was marked *Sent* but not *Delivered*. Yep, blocked.

Des's heart began to race and she forgot all about being on the clock. For the last three years, it had never been difficult to protect her heart from the women she hooked up with to forget the pain of losing Adrienne. She'd never been tempted to fall for a single one of them. And then Haley showed up and Des knew she was in trouble from the very first time their eyes locked.

They had two weeks together and those were simultaneously the best and the most painful two weeks Des'd had in a long time. She broke down all her walls for Haley. Opened herself completely to her, in more ways than one. She loved her.

And now she was going to lose her over a dumb misunderstanding.

"Hell no," she said, shoving her phone back in her pocket and leaving the string lights for someone else to put away. She knew a good thing when she had it. And she knew when to fight for it.

23
HALEY

The week went by in a slog, where every step was like wading through quicksand. Haley'd had her heart broken before – she knew how to wallow, how to shamefully eat an entire carton of ice cream and add a stomachache to her list of problems, and then throw out memories of her ex along with the evidence.

With Des, it should have been easier. It was only two weeks, and it wasn't even real – at least for one of them.

But for some reason, it hurt now more than ever. She couldn't even bring herself to go to the grocery store, load up on junk, and start the wallowing process. Probably because she knew it was her own fault for inviting the pain.

On Friday morning, she was still moving at half-speed and she had absolutely nothing to bring to the table in the weekly pitch meeting. Her well was dry, her creativity shriveled just like her heart. It was the first time since she'd started at *Traverse* that she wouldn't have a bright idea for Art when it was her turn to speak.

She was worrying over that as she got into the elevator in the lobby, and Val stepped in beside her. "Good morning!"

"You're chipper today," Haley observed.

"You still look glum," Val replied, passing her a cup of coffee and then sliding her hand into her coat pocket. But not before Haley caught a glimpse of something shiny.

"What was that?"

"What?"

"On your hand!"

"Nothing." Val reached for the elevator button, tapping it awkwardly with one knuckle of the hand holding her own coffee rather than take her hand back out of her pocket.

"Bullshit," Haley said, tugging on Val's coat sleeve. "What did you do last night?"

Val relented, showing Haley her hand. A grin spread across her face, though it looked like she was trying to suppress it. "I got engaged!"

The diamond on her finger was modest, but definitely not cheap. It looked elegant and it shined just like Val's eyes.

"Oh my god! Congratulations!" Haley pulled her into a hug as the elevator ascended.

"I wasn't sure if I should tell you," Val admitted. "Considering..." She didn't need to finish that sentence.

Haley pulled her back to arm's length so she could look at her. "Thank you for thinking of me, but that's ridiculous. Of course I want to know when my best friend gets engaged – I'm happy for you! Did you propose to Moska?"

"No, she asked me!"

They spent the rest of the elevator ride – ten floors up – talking about the proposal and admiring Val's ring. Haley already knew about the belated Valentine's date Moska had planned, and Val told her how incredibly romantic it had been – candlelight, flowers, chocolate fondue. And it had ended with the ring now adorning Val's finger, Moska asking her to be her wife.

"I guess she was ready after all!" she said, admiring her new jewelry. It perfectly encapsulated Val's personality – Moska knew her bride, that was for sure.

"Actually, she bought the ring while we were on Emerald Mountain," Val explained. "She said she missed me so much it made her realize she didn't want to spend another Valentine's Day apart."

Haley grinned, relieved to have her bad mood shunted aside at least for the moment. "Well, in that case, let's pray Art never finds out he was partially responsible – we can't afford for his ego to get any bigger."

They walked down the hallway toward the meeting room, and Val pulled Haley into a detour to the breakroom when she spotted a pink box of donuts on the counter. They each grabbed one, although Haley hadn't had much appetite lately, and Val asked, "Do you think there's any chance Des has a good excuse for what you saw?"

Haley scowled.

"Seriously," Val insisted. "Everyone in this office can see how miserably lovesick you are, and I've never seen you act like you did with her – it was like you became a different person, a better one."

"Hey."

"I'm just being honest," Val said. "That's what friends are for."

Haley sighed. "I've thought about it a lot over the past week." She stuffed a bite of blueberry cake donut into her cheek to avoid having to keep talking. Ordinarily her favorite, it tasted like gluey nothingness. Everything had this week.

"And?" Val prompted.

"It's possible," Haley said grudgingly. "Maybe there's a rational explanation, or maybe she never really cared about me after all. Maybe she's just a really good liar. I've been fooled before."

"Some people are shitty," Val agreed. "And you know I'm the first person waiting in line to kick some ass when someone hurts you. But I don't know if Des is like that."

Haley looked at her skeptically. "Did she get to you or something? Track you down online and beg you to talk to me?"

Val shook her head. "I just don't want to see you hurting. I want to see you happy like you were at the resort."

"Well, then, you should probably skip the staff meeting this morning," Haley said. "I've got nothing and Art is going to rip me a new one."

As they turned out of the break room, Val leaned in and whispered, "I've heard rumors Art's retiring at the end of the season – he might not be around to terrorize us much longer."

"That'd be one good thing in my life," Haley murmured back.

The staff meeting was tense. They happened every single week and always ran the same way, so Haley knew exactly when her moment of evisceration would come. She spent the first twenty minutes desperately trying to think of a pitch – every contributing staff member was responsible for bringing one, and it was rare for anyone to come unprepared. There were hundreds of writers and photographers in the city eager to take their place if they didn't bring their A game.

So, when it was finally Haley's turn, she put on her most confident smile and pitched an idea that had been rejected once before – a tour of the national parks and trails in Illinois that Art said was too generic an idea the first time around.

"Didn't you already suggest this?" Art asked, a deep crease between his brows.

"I don't think so," Haley lied. "I had a similar idea six months ago, but this is new." Lie, lie, lie.

Fortunately, Art had another meeting to get to and he spared her his disgust at the low-effort idea. "Pass. Val, what do you have?"

Haley let out a sigh of relief and walked out of the conference room fifteen minutes later feeling at least a little bit lighter. The weekend was right around the corner and she'd bought herself another week to pull herself together. She might have gotten lucky this week, but there was no way Art would tolerate that kind of crap two weeks in a row.

"Off the chopping block," Val whispered as they went to their desks.

"Thank God for small favors," Haley added.

When she got back to her desk, though, she went from relieved to surprised and confused. Sitting smack in the center of her desk was a small canvas on an easel, a familiar painting of lovebirds on a tree branch – or blobs, as Des had called them. Along with the canvas, there was a glass vase filled with a pretty, elaborate floral arrangement, and a note with her name on it.

Haley turned to Val. "Do you know what this is?"

Val shook her head. "Looks like Des's piece from the paint-and-sip night."

"Yeah, it is," Haley agreed, eyeing her friend suspiciously. "You swear you didn't have anything to do with this?"

"No, Scout's honor."

"You weren't a Scout," Haley pointed out. Then she asked a couple people sitting nearby who hadn't been in the staff meeting, "Did you see who left these here?"

"The receptionist set them up," one of them said. "Must have been dropped off."

Well, that was no help. Not that she was genuinely flummoxed about whose painting that was.

"Open the note," Val urged.

"I will if you stop breathing on my neck," Haley said, and Val took a respectful step back.

Haley's heart was racing as she picked up the envelope. Her name was printed on it in handwriting that was clearly Des's, although a much more careful version than she'd used to quickly scrawl the note on their first morning. Haley opened the envelope and found a card inside, a more professionally rendered bird printed on linen cardstock. She opened it.

I loved you even when I thought I wasn't capable of loving again, and I will continue loving you no matter what. Please meet me so I can clear things up – I know how hard it was for you to love again too, and I would never betray you or hurt you.

Below that, there was a time and an address, arrangements for a private car, and Des's signature.

Warmth flooded Haley's veins, just like it had every time she so much as caught a glimpse of Des on Emerald Mountain. Those words were exactly what she'd wanted to hear, and she couldn't imagine anyone going to such great lengths just to keep a side piece interested. Des was actually here, in Chicago, for her.

She looked up at Val. "Did I fuck this up? Did I let my fear get the best of me and try to push away a woman who loves me?"

Val gave her a sympathetic look which was more

answer than anything she could have said. She asked, "What does the note say?"

Haley handed it to her, and Val scanned it quickly.

"You haven't fucked up yet," she said, handing it back. "But you have to show up tonight or you could really lose her."

24
DES

*T*he closer it got to six o'clock – the time she'd asked Haley to meet her – the more nervous Des became. What if Des had miscalculated and what she'd done hadn't been enough? Flowers and a note were no grand gesture, but she hoped they were enough to get Haley to show up, to speak to her again.

When she realized she'd been blocked, Des had immediately called Joy and told her what happened. And she told her about the terrible optics the two of them had created during Joy's surprise homecoming. Of course that would look bad to a woman who'd just fallen for a self-confessed playgirl.

Joy was... less than sympathetic. "I'm sorry for my part in it, but you're the dummy who let her walk away in the first place."

"What? You told me not to smother her!" Des shot back.

"I did, but everybody knows when you love somebody, you don't let them get on an airplane and fly away," Joy answered.

"It's not too late," Des could hear Carmen chiming in from the background, then Joy put her on speakerphone. "Go now – win her back."

"Do you think I can?" Des asked.

"Do you love her?" Carmen retorted.

And Des's answer was an immediate, resounding, "Yes."

The first thing she did was head to Greg's office to tell him she quit.

"I know it's rude not to give notice, but–"

Greg interrupted her. "It's okay, really. You and I both knew you weren't going to be a lifer here at the resort, and it sounds like you're leaving me in the lurch for a good cause."

"You're a good guy, Greg," Des told him, shaking his hand.

He grinned and said, "I expect to be able to use the two of you in my promotional materials – you fell in love during my Valentine's extravaganza, after all."

Des just laughed and shook her head, not sure if he was being serious or not. "I'm sorry I wasn't always the best employee. I know how much you care about this resort, and I hope you find a replacement for me who loves it like you do."

Greg nodded. "Actually, I was thinking Ivan might be ready for some additional responsibility."

"Ivan's a good pick," Des agreed.

"Now get out of my resort," Greg teased. "Go get your Valentine."

And so, she had – or at least, she'd done everything she needed to win Haley back, as fast as she could. And a few days later, she was standing in the living room of a beautiful little secluded cabin on Pistakee Lake, about an hour outside of Chicago and the closest match she could find to an Emerald Mountain cabin, where all the magic had happened. She had the drapes pulled aside and she was anxiously waiting to see Haley coming down the driveway.

Des had taken care of everything, from the lodging to the transportation, and their dinner if she could convince Haley to stay. Now she just had to hope she'd done enough to get her here.

After what felt like a lifetime, Des heard car tires crunching up the gravel drive. Then the Town Car she'd hired pulled up to the cabin and Des's heart leapt into her throat. She let the curtains fall back and went outside, where the driver was opening Haley's door.

She was in work slacks and a button-up shirt, and she'd traded her heavy red parka for a gray wool pea coat. When she looked up at Des standing on the porch, Des's stomach did a flip. Haley was every bit as gorgeous and mesmerizing here as she was on Emerald Mountain, and Des wanted nothing more than to run down the steps and lift Haley into her arms.

She figured that wouldn't be appreciated, though, so instead, she let Haley come to her.

"Hi," she said as she reached the bottom step.

"Hi. Thanks for meeting me," Des answered. Then she nodded at the Town Car. "The driver will stay for a little while in case you want to go home, but I hope that won't be the case."

God, that was the last thing Des wanted, but she also didn't want Haley to feel like she was trapped here, in a cabin in the woods with a woman she hated. Hopefully, she wouldn't hate Des much longer.

"Thank you," Haley said, then looked around. "This cabin is beautiful. Did you rent it?"

Des nodded. "Found it on AirBNB. Apparently, it's really popular and I got lucky that there was a cancellation."

The log cabin had an extensive deck out back, wood paneling throughout, and the only two things Des really cared about – a fireplace and a great view. Of a lake this time, instead of a mountainside.

"Want to come in?" she asked, holding out her hand.

Haley took it, even though the porch steps were swept and she didn't really need Des's help. Des waved to the driver, who pulled up to a parking spot away from the front door. He'd be okay out there for the next thirty minutes, and if Haley hadn't decided to leave by then, Des had instructed him that he could go.

Inside the cabin, Des already had a fire crackling on the hearth, a big, fuzzy blanket on the couch for cozying up – she was thinking optimistically when she got ready for the evening. Sitting in ice on the dining table was a bottle of champagne – another optimistic touch – and the kitchen was all set up with the ingredients for red velvet waffles, the recipe the two of them had learned to make at the resort.

To top it all off, Des had put on her best suit, the one she rarely had cause to take out of her closet, and paired it with a greenish-blue bowtie to match her hair.

Haley swept her eyes over all of it, drinking it in, and last of all, she looked at Des. There was a definite sparkle of hope in her eyes, telling Des all was not lost. But she could tell Haley had her guard up.

Deep breath, here goes.

Des stepped forward and took Haley's hand. "I'm so glad you're here with me. Hell, even if you're mad at me, I'm over the moon just to be in the same state with you again."

That earned her a small smile.

"For the first couple of days after you left, I was so worried that you weren't answering me," Des went on. "I even convinced myself your plane crashed and I had terrible images in my head."

Haley frowned. "I'm sorry. I was upset, but I didn't mean to scare you."

"Well, eventually I put two and two together and figured out you must have seen me hugging Joy, right?"

Haley's expression darkened. "Is that her name?"

"There's never been anything romantic between me and her," Des rushed on. "She's my friend – remember the one I told you about, who used to work at the resort and left to travel the country with her girlfriend? She came to visit, and she's not shy about expressing her feelings."

"So she's only a friend?" Haley asked.

Des nodded. "I swear on my life ,and I made her and Carmen – who's her wife now – record a video on my phone to introduce themselves to you. Carmen's twelve weeks pregnant, by the way, and they both wanted to meet you. That's why they came. Do you want to see the video?"

She pulled her phone out of her pocket, but Haley shook her head. "Maybe later," she said. "Shit, I am such an idiot."

Des took a step closer. She was close enough now to reach out and brush Haley's arm, and she did. When

Haley made no move to pull away, Des wrapped her in a hug. "You are not an idiot. You've just had your heart broken before and you were protecting yourself."

"Pushing you away," Haley confessed. "I'm sorry."

"Me too," Des said. "I hate that you spent the past week thinking I was some playgirl who didn't care about you. And I hate that I didn't do enough while you were on the mountain to prove that isn't who I am anymore."

"And I hate that I'm still so afraid of a good thing that I'm willing to sabotage it all," Haley added.

Des pulled back a little bit and tilted Haley's chin up to meet her gaze. "Hey, we're both a little broken when it comes to love... but we can spend the rest of our lives mending each other. If that's what you want."

"The rest of our lives?" Haley's eyes were full of stars now, and Des couldn't quite tell if they were tears or just overflowing emotion.

Des smiled. "Hell, you didn't think I did all of this just to apologize, did you?" She reached into the inside pocket of her jacket and pulled out a ring box. Haley drew in a sharp breath.

"Des–"

"You don't want to leave, do you? Because I don't think the driver's gonna stick around much longer."

Now there were definite tears pooling in Haley's

eyes as she shook her head. "I don't want to be anywhere but here... with you."

Des held the ring box in her hand, tapping it against the opposite palm. The words – *will you marry me, Haley Thomas?* – had been biting at the back of her throat since the minute she picked out the ring. But before she could ask that question, she had to be sure that Haley knew exactly how much she was loved. And how eternal that love was.

"I would have kept trying if this didn't work, you know," Des said. "If you didn't show up, or if you did but you didn't like my explanation, I had backup plans. I wasn't going to stop trying until you knew without a shadow of a doubt that I love you and that I'm yours – no one else's – forever. I would have hired a skywriter if I had to."

Haley laughed. "I'm glad it didn't go that far – I bet that would be expensive."

"You're worth it." Des pulled Haley close to her again, closing her fists around her hips, drawing their bodies together. "I've already lost one love of my life, and until I met you, I never thought I would have that kind of love again. I didn't think I was that lucky. But now that I've met you, and held you, and loved you... I'm sure as hell not letting you go."

25

HALEY

*D*es nudged Haley's cheek with her nose, the intoxicating smell of her making Haley dizzy with desire – not just for sex, but for Des herself.

Her destiny.

"I don't want to push you away anymore, but I can't promise I won't do it again," she confessed. "It's ingrained at this point, like a reflex."

"Push me away a thousand times," Des said. "As long as I know that you love me, that you want me, I'll pull you right back."

"And the thousand-and-first time?"

"Thousandth, millionth, doesn't matter," Des said. "I will never stop loving you and pursuing you." Then she held the ring box up. At last, she cracked it open and inside, Haley saw a perfectly round, icy-blue stone on a gold band.

"It's beautiful."

"I wanted to pick something unique, like you," Des explained. "This one reminded me of the mountain, of the snow, and your eyes. Plus, aquamarines are good luck charms for long, pleasant journeys... which is what I hope the rest of our lives together will be."

Haley gave a half smile. "You haven't actually asked yet."

Des grinned back. "I was getting there. Sheesh, don't rush my proposal."

"I'm sorry." Haley couldn't have wiped the smile from her face now if she tried.

Her heart was pounding as Des presented the ring to her again and said, "Haley Thomas, I love you with every ounce of my heart, mind and soul. I don't want to be apart from you for another minute, and I never want you to have a moment of doubt about how damn much I want you. Will you be my wife?"

A giggle rose up Haley's throat. "This is crazy. We've known each other less than a month."

"We'll have a long engagement," Des said, then shrugged. "Or not. We know our own hearts, right?"

"Yes."

"In any case, I'm sure Greg would be thrilled to host our wedding at the resort – it'd make for great PR," Des said. "So... what's your answer?"

"Of course I want to marry you," Haley said.

"You're my Valentine – this year and every year. I knew I wanted you to be mine since the moment Cupid struck me with his arrow."

"And when was that?" Des teased, taking the ring out of the box and sliding it onto Haley's finger. "When you saw me up on that ladder?"

Haley grinned. It was her turn to be coy. "Well, I thought you were hot as hell then – I definitely wanted to bang you. But I knew I was falling in love with you the night you shared your favorite place in the resort with me. That's when I really started to see who you were, and I loved everything I saw." She admired the ring on her finger. "It's a perfect fit."

Des grinned. "I may have tracked Val down on social media and asked her to help out with a few things, including your ring size."

"I knew it!" Haley shrieked. "And she did such a good job of playing dumb when that painting showed up on my desk. I'm gonna kill her."

Des laughed. "Please tell me we can burn that painting now. It's done its duty, time to put the blobs out of their misery."

"Hell no," Haley said. "I put mine in my closet when I got home, but now that the paintings are reunited, just like us, they're getting pride of place above my mantel."

Des laughed, then scooped Haley into her arms,

lifting her off her feet. Haley wrapped her legs around Des's hips and clung to her as they kissed – deep, passionate, like it'd been a year since they last saw each other instead of a week. Then Des said, "And speaking of mantels... what do you think of the cabin? I rented it for the weekend. I figured we could get cozy by the fire tonight, make red velvet waffles, get sticky with syrup... lick it off each other..."

"Mmm, I like the sound of that. When do you have to go back to Emerald Mountain?"

Des was walking Haley over to the fireplace. She laid her down on top of a heap of cushions and blankets, then crawled between her thighs. "I don't."

Haley paused, propped up on her elbows. "You don't?"

"I told Greg my life was in Chicago and I had to leave immediately to win you back," she said. "I quit my job, which, I'll be honest, I wasn't trying all that hard to be good at in the first place. I'll find another one here in the city... if that's what you want."

Haley cracked up. "What I want? I've got your ring on my finger."

"Well, like you said – it's been less than a month," Des said. "If you want some space, if you want me to go back to Emerald Hill for a while–"

"Hey, this has been the best less-than-a-month of my life," Haley said, wrapping her legs around Des's hips again and hooking her ankles together behind her back. "Of course I want you to stay. I don't want you going anywhere... especially right now. Can we freeze time here?"

Des kissed her, letting the length of her body down against Haley's, savoring the feeling. "Unfortunately, we can't do that... but we can press 'repeat' as many times as we want, for the rest of our lives."

"I love it when you push my buttons," Haley teased, squirming and grinding her hips beneath her as warmth bloomed between her legs. "Des?"

"Yes, Haley?"

"Fuck my brains out."

Des grinned. "I've been waiting all week to hear those words."

She raised onto her knees and her hands traveled down Haley's body, from her jawline down the length of her neck, and over the mounds of her breasts. Haley felt her nipples hardening beneath Des's touch and she tightened her thighs around her, squirming with need.

"Touch me," she begged. It felt like a lifetime since she last had Des's body pressed up against her own. She stripped off her shirt and shimmied out of her bra, and Des wasted no time enveloping her breasts in her hands, then bending to take them in her mouth one at a time.

Her tongue swirled over Haley's nipples, and she

nibbled softly on the delicate skin, heating Haley's body to the point of delirium.

She reached up and grabbed Des's shirt collar, ditching the bowtie and then working the buttons loose as fast as she could. "I need you naked on top of me," she groaned, her clit throbbing and every nerve tingling.

"I can't argue with that," Des grinned.

She rose to her knees again and tossed her shirt aside, then pulled off her undershirt and threw that away, too. Her hair fell over her eyes, and the hunger in her gaze looked more animal than woman – it sent an excited little shiver down Haley's spine and she had to bite her lip to contain it.

"God, I've missed you."

"Me too," Des said, making short work of her pants and underwear. "We never have to be apart again now."

She grabbed hold of Haley's work slacks. Haley had just enough time to unbutton them before Des yanked them down her legs, damn near dragging Haley along with them. Haley laughed, then grabbed Des by the back of the neck and pulled her down to the blanket.

Her body was warm, her skin soft and her muscles firm in all the right places. Haley could feel Des's abs tense against her core as she wrapped her thighs around her again, and she used the grip of her legs to roll them both to the side. The fireplace was nearby, letting off just the right amount of heat to keep them comfy, but Haley had another heat source on her mind. She slipped one hand into the tight space between their bodies, and into the slickness of Des's folds.

"You're so wet," she grinned, slipping one finger teasingly into her.

"Who's fucking who?" Des asked.

"Whom," Haley said.

"Nerd."

Haley shrugged. "Can't help it, my best friend is a writer."

Des growled, then pounced, pushing Haley onto her stomach. "How dare you think of another woman right now," she chastised. She took Haley by the wrists and planted them on either side of her head, pinning her in place. Then she bent down, her hot breath and pert nipples barely brushing Haley's back as she whispered, "Mine's the only name I want coming out of your mouth tonight."

Haley's thighs squeezed together involuntarily, a spasm working its way through her core at the idea. "I'm yours. Forever."

"My pretty little Valentine," Des said, nipping at Haley's earlobe. "I'm gonna make you scream my name."

And then Haley felt a hand on her ass, caressing one cheek before venturing lower, into the wetness that was practically pooling between her legs now. "Yes... yes, Des, make me come," she murmured, already feeling a little out of breath.

Des plunged two fingers into Haley's core, pumping in and out of her, sending the most delicious sensations through her with every thrust. And while she did it, she kissed and licked her way down Haley's bare back, tickling and teasing with every touch. Haley pushed up onto her hands and knees for leverage, rocking her hips back against Des's hand in time with her thrusts. Des looped her free hand around Haley's waist, finding her clit.

"Oooooh, fuck!" Haley groaned, barely able to form words.

"That feel good, baby?"

"Yes," she panted, bouncing harder against Des's hand.

"I have something that might feel even better," she said, her hand disappearing from Haley's clit. Haley was just about to pout about that when a fat silicone dildo appeared in her peripheral vision, Des holding it out for her approval. "What do you think?"

It was a double-ended little number, and Haley couldn't help commenting on the obvious. "It's bright pink. I didn't take you for a pink sex toy kinda girl."

"I'm not, normally," Des said. "But, you know, I figured it matched the Valentine's theme I was referencing. So... should I fuck you with it?"

The words sent a quiver of need through Haley's body and she felt herself clenching around Des's fingers.

"Mmm, feels like you want me to."

Haley bucked her hips a couple of times in agreement. "God, yes. Fill me up. Fuck me hard."

"Yes, ma'am," Des said. Her fingers withdrew and Haley's body gave an instant cry of revolt. She and Des had only known each other for such a short time, but being with her felt more natural than anything else in her whole life. The absence of her, even if only for a moment, was torture.

Haley flipped onto her back so she could drink in the view. She kept her thighs spread and she circled a finger over her own clit while she watched Des open her own legs wider, lubing the dildo with her own juices before sliding it in. Haley grinned hungrily up at her. "Does that feel good?"

"Yeah," Des agreed, barely able to tear her eyes away from Haley's hand on her own body. "Gonna feel even better when the other end is inside you. Come here, baby."

Haley welcomed her into the space between her thighs. Her pussy was already throbbing with need for release, and her whole body shook each time Des guided the dildo up and down Haley's folds, over her hardened clit, getting it wet and ready.

And then, she pushed into her.

"Oh, fuck!" Haley threw her head back, her voice echoing off the wood-beamed ceiling.

"Say my name," Des begged as she drew back, then pushed in as far as she could go, until their hips met.

"Des!" Haley was only too happy to oblige. "Fuck me, Des!"

And Des didn't hold back. She grabbed Haley's hips and thrust into her again, making each long, hard stroke count. Each one brought Haley closer to the edge, and she could feel Des's pace quickening as her own arousal built.

Then, just before Haley reached the peak, Des pulled back and reached between them. She had one more trick up her sleeve, pressing a concealed button molded into the silicone. Vibration exploded into Haley's core and Des followed it up with another swift thrust into her.

The sensation overwhelmed her, overrode circuits in her brain, made her incapable of language, of anything other than riding out the most intense orgasm of her life. At some point, Haley couldn't single it out, Des started to come too. She fell forward, bracing herself on either side of Haley's shoulders, bucking and grinding her hips against their shared toy.

Haley laced her ankles behind Des's back, pulling them tight, locking them in mutual ecstasy. Haley's body took over then, grinding along with Des and giving herself over completely to the moment.

To Des.

Her destiny.

Her future wife.

26
DES

Christmastime on Emerald Mountain was totally different from Valentine's Day. They each had their charm, and Valentine's Day would always have a special place in Des's heart for obvious reasons, but she was excited to share a whole new holiday with Haley here in her hometown.

She'd been back a handful of times since that first visit to Chicago – to take care of practical details like packing her things and subletting her apartment, to visit her parents on their birthdays. But this was the first time since last Valentine's Day that Haley was able to come with her.

Des had moved to Chicago right away, and she'd started her own handywoman business. The first couple of months were challenging because she didn't know anyone in the city, but once her first client started raving about her online, the work orders began flooding in. She'd gotten to know Val and her fiancée, Moska, and they double-dated all the time.

They were perfect together, like strawberries and mascarpone, and even their parents had to agree that they'd never seen two people more in love, more in sync. Even if both sets of parental units had been initially alarmed at how quickly the relationship had developed.

"I hope you're planning on a long engagement," Haley's father had warned the first time she brought Des home to meet them. It wasn't that he didn't like Des – she'd brought him a Colorado microbrew and he'd instantly turned warm and chatty. He was just a pragmatist, and protective of his daughter. Des could respect that.

Haley's mother, however, had pulled Des aside just before they left that night. She'd clutched Des's hand in the hallway while Haley's dad walked her out to the car and said, "Falling fast isn't always falling foolishly. I knew I wanted to marry Haley's father the minute I laid eyes on him. Of course, it took him another year and a half to come around on that... you and Haley are at least on the same page."

Des had laughed. "Does that mean I have your blessing?"

"I wouldn't give it to just anyone, but even in the

short time I've known you, I can tell how much my daughter loves you, and how much you love her," she said. "All I want is for Haley to be happy. Can you make her happy?"

"I'm going to spend the rest of my life trying," Des promised.

"Then you have my wholehearted blessing," the elder Thomas woman said, patting Des's hand.

"Hey, what are you two doing in there?" Haley called from the driveway.

"Nothing, coming," her mom called back, then gave Des a conspiratorial wink. They'd been thick as thieves ever since.

Haley had been wearing Des's ring for nine months now, and everything was going better than Des could have expected. Their wedding plans were well underway, and they'd come to Emerald Mountain on a triple mission: introduce Haley to Des's parents, celebrate Christmas, and make a few last-minute arrangements for their wedding.

They chose the resort for practical reasons – Greg promised to give them a hefty discount if he could parade their success story all over the resort's social media accounts. And they'd chosen the date – Valentine's Day – for sentimental ones.

Des and Haley met her parents at an upscale steakhouse in Emerald Hill their first night in town. They had a great meal followed by incredible desserts, and Haley charmed Des's parents just like Des knew she would.

"I just can't believe you won't stay at our house," her mom said in the parking lot as they prepared to part ways for the evening. "Your bedroom is just how you left it."

Des laughed. "And I told you years ago you could reclaim it. It's not like I'm moving home anytime soon."

"Well, you always have a place with us if you need it," her mom answered, then put her hand on Haley's arm. "That goes for you too now, soon-to-be daughter-in-law."

As intriguing as it was to think about snuggling up next to Haley in her childhood bed, it wasn't how Des wanted to spend the next week. For one, it was a single mattress. And an entire week of lying next to Haley but knowing she couldn't risk touching her because her parents' headboard was right on the other side of the wall? No thanks.

It was Christmas, after all, and Des intended to kiss Haley under the mistletoe every chance she got.

"We're fine at the resort, Mom," she assured her. "I want Haley to get the full Emerald Mountain Christmas experience. Besides, she's never skied the moguls before and I promised her we'd tackle them."

"Okay, but you're coming over in the afternoon tomorrow to bake Christmas cookies, right?" she asked.

"Wouldn't miss it," Haley said with another one of her mom-charming grins. It was like she'd been a member of the family for years, and even Adrienne hadn't gotten along with Des's parents this quickly. Des could already imagine a lifetime of Christmases, vacations, and even the quiet moments together with Haley.

And someday, kids.

Joy and Carmen were four months into parenthood and pestering the two of them to hurry up and start their own family so their kids could grow up together. They'd named their first child Chase because Carmen's labor was unexpectedly quick, and they were already anticipating he'd be a tough kid to keep up with.

"It'll be a couple more years before we get him on tiny little skis," Joy had said over the phone one day. "That's plenty of time for you and Haley to catch up with a little one of your own."

Des had just laughed. "We're not even married yet – slow down!"

"Why? You two certainly didn't go slow when you met."

"And neither did you and Carmen," Des pointed

out. "I guess there's something about the mountain air that makes you appreciate the moment."

On their second day back at the resort, Des and Haley met the caterers for a dry run of the wedding reception menu they'd chosen, and then they tasted half a dozen wedding cake options. There was the usual fare – vanilla, chocolate, almond – but the last cake the baker brought out was special, a request Des had made in secret.

"And finally, we have a custom option," she said, setting two dessert plates down in front of them. "I made this recipe three different times before I was sure I got it right, and it's so good I'm considering putting it on the resort restaurant menu."

Haley's eyes lit up when she saw the strawberry-topped cake slices. "What is it?"

"Strawberry-mascarpone filling in a white cake, with a dark chocolate drizzle," the baker, Harmony, said. Des had her eyes on Haley, who appeared to be suppressing drool.

She looked at Des. "Did you have a hand in this?"

Des smiled. "Guilty as charged. I know how much you loved the berries from Valentine's Day."

"Well, I don't even need to taste it – this cake gets my vote," Haley said, picking up her fork. "But I will taste it... for science."

Des picked up her own fork. "For science."

They clinked their silverware together like champagne flutes and dug in. Haley's eyes fluttered shut as she savored the cake, and Des let out an indecent groan before she could stop herself. Harmony grinned and said, "I take it you've made your selection?"

"Yep, and we'll also take any extra slices you may have off your hands," Des said, then gave Haley a wink. "For later."

Once they were finished with their wedding-related tasks for the day, they'd been planning to head out to the slopes and conquer the moguls. But Haley put a hand on her stomach and puffed out her cheeks. "I know we only tasted everything, but I feel like I ate a four-course meal. Not sure a bumpy ski slope is the best idea right now."

"Why don't we go to the lounge, curl up in front of a fireplace and digest a while?" Des suggested.

"That's a good idea," Haley agreed. "I need maybe an hour, and then you can teach me to navigate the moguls."

So they dropped off the extra cake slices they'd managed to wrest from Harmony, then headed to the lounge. It was a little busier than the last time the two of them were there, but the mountain had just gotten a fresh dusting of powder and a lot of people were outside enjoying it. That left Des and Haley with plenty of room to stretch out in a plush loveseat by the fire.

"Want a cup of coffee?" Des asked.

Haley nodded, and Des went over to the bar to order the drinks. When she came back, Haley held out her hands for the coffee cup. Des settled in beside her, her fiancée feeling absolutely snuggly in an oversized knit sweater. Haley asked, "Remember the last time we were here? That time, it was hot cocoa by the bar."

Des nodded. "With heart-shaped marshmallows."

Haley looked in her cup, then grinned back at her. Floating on top of her coffee was a heart-shaped cloud. "How did you pull this off?"

"I know a guy," Des said with a shrug. "Anyway, that's frozen whipped cream, not a marshmallow. Much better pair for coffee."

She handed Haley a spoon to stir it, then wrapped her arm around Haley's shoulder. Haley snuggled in. "You're the best... strawberry-mascarpone cake and little hearts in my coffee... I don't deserve you."

Des hooked Haley's chin, turning her head so she could look into Haley's eyes. "Don't ever say that – you deserve every good thing in the world and it's my job to make sure you get it."

"Well, I can think of a thing or two that I'd like to give you," Haley answered, leaning in for a kiss. Her lips were sweet and rich with the taste of whipped cream.

"Oh yeah?"

"What do you say we skip the moguls for today and go see if your favorite spot is still as you left it?" Haley said, softly so no one nearby would overhear.

"I like that idea," Des said. "You still too full?"

"Not for that."

"Well, what are we waiting for?" Des kissed Haley, sneaking a quick squeeze of her breast through her sweater. She felt Haley's nipple harden, and suddenly she couldn't get up to the attic fast enough. "God, I love you."

"I love you too, Des," Haley breathed against her mouth. "Forever."

EPILOGUE

HALEY

*V*alentine's Day was known for its romance, but for Haley, it was so much more than just chocolates in heart-shaped boxes and cheesy greeting cards and an excuse to buy jewelry. That might have been how she thought of it before, but from this day on, it would forever be the best day of the year.

The holiday that led her to her soulmate.

The season of falling head over heels.

The day she became Des's wife.

Haley was dressed in a beaded, shimmering gown that clinked softly when she moved, and she'd had a hell of a time sneaking over to Des's dressing room for that reason. She was in the hallway now, right outside the door. She could hear Des inside with her mom, Joy and Carmen, putting the finishing touches on her wedding suit. Haley could picture it – they'd picked it out together. It had a beaded bodice, a touch of femininity amid the more masculine cut of the rest of the crisp white suit.

It was perfect for Des, and it also perfectly complemented Haley's gown – and she couldn't wait to see all the wedding photos. In fact, the photographer part of her wished she could be two people for the day. One who was getting married to the love of her life, and another that got to experience the whole thing from behind her camera lens, capturing the moment for eternity.

Considering cloning was not in the cards, they'd decided on the much more practical step of hiring a wedding photographer, splurging for the best one in the area. But Haley wasn't content to keep her own photography completely out of the mix – that was why she was standing in the hallway, listening in on her future wife.

She knocked on the door, praying Des didn't answer it herself. She wanted to hear Des's reaction, so she couldn't send a messenger, but she still wanted their photographer to capture their first looks at each other as they joined at the altar. So, Haley had done the only reasonable thing and looped Joy in on the mission.

And Joy followed through. She beat Des to the

door, opening it just wide enough for Haley to pass a package through.

"Thanks," she whispered.

Joy nodded, then left the door open a crack so Haley could hear better. She went back across the room to Des, saying, "Special delivery."

"What's this?" Haley heard Des ask. There were the sounds of the package being opened – it was butcher paper over a copy of *Traverse,* tied with a ribbon in their wedding color, teal to match Des's hair, and finished off with a note.

The magazine issue was the one Haley and Val had been working on when they first came to the mountain. A year later, the Valentine's feature had finally run, and Haley's photo of the pristine, snow-covered mountains, with Des's pink string lights in the foreground, had been selected for the cover. What was more important, though, was the page she'd bookmarked inside.

Haley heard page-flipping and pictured Des reading the note.

I finally got my cover photo, but what's even more important to me is that the magazine selected this photo of you for the inside feature. Art saw the beauty in it the same way I did. This is the very first picture I ever took of you, and you took my breath away – behind the lens and then again in person. I can't wait to spend the rest of my life stealing candid shots of you and having my breath stolen in return.

"Did Haley deliver this?" Des asked Joy.

"You can't see her yet," Carmen reminded her.

"Like hell I can't," Des answered, and then there was a bit of shuffling. Haley thought she even heard Joy trying to block Des's path, and then the door flew open. Des encircled Haley in her arms, pushing her up against the wall, kissing her fiercely in the hallway.

Haley lost sight of everyone else, giving herself over to the kiss. She breathed in Des's woodsy, lavender scent and struggled to keep her fingers out of her carefully styled hair. That would come later – Haley couldn't wait to muss Des's hair and tear off her suit the minute they got back to their cabin after the reception.

Which seemed like so far away in this moment.

When they finally came up for air, Haley heard a camera shutter and turned her head. Their photographer was standing at the other end of the hallway, and she peeked her head over the camera lens. "It's not a traditional first look, but it's gonna make for some great prints." She grinned and added, "Maybe more on the boudoir side than most people have."

"Well, we're not most people," Des said, then turned back to Haley. "You ready to get married?"

"I've never been more ready for anything," Haley

answered, taking her hand. "Come on, I need to make you my wife as well as my Valentine."

AUTHOR'S NOTE

Hello!

Thank you so much for reading *Destiny* – I had so much fun returning to Emerald Mountain so I hope you loved Des and Haley as much as I do.

If you haven't read Carmen and Joy's Christmas romance yet, check it out here:

Read *Joy: Christmas on Emerald Mountain* in Kindle Unlimited.

Have a great day and happy reading!

—*Cara*

facebook.com/caramalonebooks
twitter.com/caramalonebooks
goodreads.com/caramalonebooks
bookbub.com/authors/cara-malone

Printed in Great Britain
by Amazon